oki

SE

P

MISSING

SUSPENSE

MISSING

THERESA BRESLIN

mammoth

First published in Great Britain 1995 by Mammoth
Reissued 1999 by Mammoth
an imprint of Egmont Children's Books Limited
239 Kensington High Street, London W8 6SA

ISBN 0 7497 1856 0

10 9 8 7 6 5 4 3 2 1

A CIP catalogue record for this title
is available from the British Library

Printed and Great Britain
by Cox & Wyman Ltd, Reading, Berkshire

ONE

MISSING TEENAGER FOUND DEAD
IN LOCAL WOOD!

Andi MacNeil pushed her fringe out of her eyes and peered more closely at the newspaper headline. 'Look.' She nudged her friend Liz. 'They've found that girl who's been missing for the last few weeks.'

'Yeah, yeah. I noticed,' said Liz without even glancing up from her magazine. 'Hanging around woods on your own is a pretty dumb thing to do.'

'But she wasn't in a wood to begin with,' persisted Andi. 'That's just where they eventually found her. She went missing somewhere else. And you'll never guess where from,' she added excitedly as she read down the column.

'Mmm . . .' said Liz. She shoved her magazine back on the rack and picked up another one. 'I give up. Where did she go missing?'

'From this very mall,' said Andi. She quoted from the newspaper; 'Police are anxious to trace the person Tracy was last seen with. He or she may have vital evidence as to how she died.' Andi

1

looked around her. She was standing just inside the entrance to the newsagent's and she had a good view all the way across the shopping precinct. She surveyed the Friday-night throng of late shoppers. Could one of these seemingly innocent passers-by be implicated in some way in Tracy's death?

'Isn't that an amazing coincidence?' she said to Liz.

'Yeah,' said Liz sarcastically. 'Absolutely amazing. This is the only shopping mall within reasonable interplanetary spaceship distance of this dull and boring town, and every teenager for two hundred miles around hangs out here, so it is fantastically incredibly amazing that this is the last place that the poor girl was seen.' She picked up another magazine and opened it.

'Are you young ladies thinking of buying a magazine today,' the newsagent called out sharply, 'or did you only come in to read your way through as many as possible before I ask you to leave?'

Liz gave him a cheeky grin. 'We just came in to read as many as we can before you throw us out,' she said.

The man slammed his till drawer shut and came out from behind the counter.

'Only joking. Only joking,' said Liz and she pulled her purse from her jeans pocket and waved it under his nose.

The newsagent laughed as he took her money. 'Cheeky madam,' he said.

'I don't know how you've got the nerve,' said

2

Andi as they walked on through the mall. 'You read about ten of his magazines every week for free.'

Liz shrugged. 'I can't help it,' she said. 'It's because I'm a Gemini. Active, inquisitive and humorous.'

'Rubbish,' said Andi. 'I've told you before. You shouldn't set your life by those horoscopes.'

'I don't let them control everything I do,' Liz argued back, 'but you shouldn't just dismiss them completely. They give valuable advice. Most great rulers have consulted astrologers at some time.'

'Yeah, and look at the state the world's in today,' said Andi. The two friends stopped and leant over the rail which circled the top-floor shopping level. The great glass dome of the mall arched above their heads and the artificial lights reflected and sparkled on its surface like coloured stars. Directly in front of them hung the Rennie Mackintosh clock, its stately pendulum ticking away the minutes. It was the middle of November and Christmas decorations were already showing in most of the shops. From where they stood they could see the big Norwegian spruce tree being erected on the lower floor.

'Only six weeks to Christmas, I can hardly believe it,' said Liz.

'Neither can I,' Andi groaned. 'I've dozens of presents to buy and I'm stony broke. Everybody has a part-time job except me.'

'I'll ask my shop manageress again tonight,' said Liz. 'They might take on more staff soon. I mean, *everyone* wants a new pair of shoes for Christmas. But you need a lot of patience, I'm telling you. If I get one more spoiled brat puking over me on a Saturday morning I may hand in my notice.'

Suddenly two brown hands grabbed the girls, one on each neck.

'Hey, beat it, you,' yelled Liz, struggling and laughing as the boy behind them pretended to push them both over the ornamental railing.

'Paul!' said Andi, smiling up at him.

'Might have known,' said Liz, breaking free and hitting him on the head with her magazine. 'On our way to do our shift at the Kookie Kounter, are we?' she asked him sweetly. 'Bet you don't get moaned at about your sales figures.'

'Can I help it if no one can resist my fatal charm, stunning good looks, excellent patter and winning ways?' Paul gave them his best smile, even white teeth gleaming in his dark handsome face. Andi and Liz pretended to faint.

'Please, please,' moaned Liz. 'I need one of Paul's special-milk-chocolate-double-kookies-with-coconut or I will die.'

Andi giggled. Paul stuck his Kookie Kounter baseball cap to the back of his head and winked at her.

'Stop by and talk to me later?' he said.

Andi flushed. 'Sure,' she said casually.

He flicked his fingers through the ends of her hair as he walked away.

'He fancies you,' said Liz as soon as he was out of earshot.

'Paul fancies anything with two bumps at the front,' said Andi at once. She sighed as she said it, but she knew it was true. He was famed over the neighbourhood for having several girls chasing after him at any one time. They wandered towards the shoe market where Liz was due to start her evening shift.

'Hey, that's new,' said Andi. She pointed to where a young woman was sitting near the top of the mall's main escalator. Her head was bent over her artist's easel, her sleek brown hair making a bell shape around her cheeks as she leant across her work.

'*Pam's Predictions*' Liz read the sign aloud. 'Looks interesting,' she said.

They moved closer to look at the poster.

Ideal and unusual Christmas gift
Pam will paint your portrait
Have it done while you wait
Or, if you have no time to spare,
Leave a photograph if you prefer.
She will also plan your own personal starscape

Liz gripped Andi's arm. 'Excellent,' she said. 'I had no idea what to get you for your birthday next month. Here is the perfect present.' She grabbed Andi's hand and started dragging her towards the new stall.

'I'm not sure.' Andi hung back, a sudden strange reluctance making her hesitate.

'For goodness sake!' said Liz. 'I don't have much time, c'mon. Anyway,' she added, 'if you really don't believe in them, then what possible effect can they have on you?'

Andi looked again at the poster, and at the woman working so intently on her painting. Astrological predictions were just so much nonsense. She had decided that years ago, despite what Liz said. So . . . there would be no harm in having hers done, would there? She followed Liz and stood behind the artist, watching her work. As they waited for the girl to stop sketching Andi read the rest of the notice.

> 'Pam's Predictions'
> *Astral Fortunes. Achieve an insight into your own personality. Thinking of a change of career? Leaving school? Knowledge of your star sign can help you.*

Andi glanced about her, rubbing her arms. Although it was almost December it wasn't at all cold in the mall.

So, why had she suddenly felt a shiver running through her?

TWO

Liz shoved Andi into the little canvas stool. 'One customer, Pam,' she called out cheerfully.

The young woman stopped sketching. She looked at them carefully and put her hand on a holdall at her feet. 'What did you want, exactly?' she asked.

'A portrait, with a special astral prediction for a soon-to-be birthday girl,' said Liz.

'Oh, of course,' said Pam lightly. She glanced round her, then inserted a clean piece of card under the clips on her easel. 'When is your birthday?' she asked Andi.

Andi felt slightly uncomfortable as the other girl scrutinised her with cool grey eyes. 'December the twentieth,' she said.

'Ah,' said Pam, 'that's almost into Capricorn. You're on the cusp.' She frowned. 'It means that you can have characteristics of both signs, Capricorn and Sagittarius. It should make you a more interesting study.' She wrote Andi's date of birth at the top left-hand side of the card. Then underneath that she deftly drew a tiny centaur holding a bow and arrow. It was rearing on its hind legs with long hair flowing back.

7

'That's good,' said Liz approvingly.

'Thanks,' said Pam. She got up and turned Andi's head slightly to one side and arranged her long blonde hair so that it fell across one shoulder. Then she pushed Andi's fringe back from her face. 'So that we can see these unusual hazel eyes,' she said. She sat down again and adjusted her easel. 'Good,' she said. 'I see you have a natural smile, so I don't have to ask you to say cheese.'

Andi relaxed slightly. Her dad always said that her sunny smile was her best feature but she didn't usually pay much attention. It was, after all, what you would expect your dad to say, and anyway she always felt as though she was a pale shadow beside Liz, who with her brown curly hair and cheeky grin usually drew more attention.

Pam chatted to Andi as she worked, asking about her likes and dislikes, interests and hobbies. She paused from time to time in her drawing to add a few lines of writing to the left of the picture.

'Nearly done,' she said. 'I'll do a few finishing touches and complete your personal prediction along the bottom under your portrait.'

'Looks brilliant,' commented Liz from her spot behind the easel.

Pam laughed. 'Well, I don't know about brilliant,' she said, 'but I think I've captured a bit of her likeness.'

'You're an art student, aren't you?' asked Liz. 'Something like that,' said Pam evasively. She wrote the number nine at the bottom edge of the page, and drew some red flames licking round it. 'There,' she said. 'Sagittarius, ninth sign of the zodiac, a fire sign and symbolised by the archer.' She completed the picture with an arrow slanting across the card.

Liz paid her and presented the completed card to Andi with a flourish. 'Happy birthday in advance,' she said.

'Thanks,' said Andi. 'It's a really unusual present. Even though,' she lowered her voice so that Pam wouldn't hear, 'I think it's all a lot of twaddle.'

'You will live to regret saying that,' said Liz dramatically. 'The power of the planets will overcome. Their signs will seek you out. Anyway,' she looked up at the mall clock, and her voice changed abruptly, 'I'd better zip along mega-fast or I'll be docked some cash for being late. See ya.' She waved and ran towards the shoe market.

Andi hung around the artist's table for a bit. It was a good place to people-watch, right next to the huge long escalators which brought shoppers up and down from the car park and café on the lower level. She nodded and called out to a few friends. They were all hurrying off to their weekend jobs, Petra in the hairdresser's, Tony in the sports shop. It seemed everybody had evening or Saturday work except her. It was partly to do with her age of course. She was one of the youngest in her year group, with her birthday falling in the winter term. It meant that most of her classmates already had their national insurance cards before her. But she had heard that some shops would employ you if you were almost sixteen. And she was, well, nearly.

She thought of her birthday, next month. Her dad had promised to buy her something different. Just being the two of them, he usually did try to make a big thing of her special day. She glanced at her watch. She'd better head home. She didn't want him coming in from the office before her and worrying when she wasn't there. She took out her portrait and studied it. Pam *had* got her likeness. The curtain of blonde hair framing her oval face. The wispy fringe above the brown eyes flecked with green. The soft full mouth shaded in pink. It was a bit eerie to look down and see yourself staring back. Creepy almost. Andi shivered again.

She would do a quick tour of the mall and then go home, she decided. She made a face at Tony through the glass window of his shop. They were changing the display and he was struggling with a set of weights and a rowing machine. The window dresser was draping a quiver of arrows over the arm of an elegant mannequin. A crossbow lay at its feet. Nice Christmas present, thought Andi. She wandered on.

One look at the little shop tucked almost in the corner and then I'm off, she decided. It was called Moonstone and it was very small. Liz didn't like it, the way everything was cramped inside, all the goods piled about in disorder. But Andi did. It sold a wide variety of handmade skirts and tops, ethnic jewellery, little coloured skull caps, bags, belts and scarves. The owner, a severe-looking man with a beard and wire glasses, always glared at young people coming in, but Andi had found that this was only if they were in groups, pushing each other, or laughing and giggling. When she went in by herself to browse he would give her a brief nod. And he never harassed her, even though she didn't always buy.

She could see that the window was badly lit as she approached it. It definitely needed a professional touch, especially for the festive season. Andi was sure he would do a lot more business if only the goods were set out properly. She peered in the window and was on the point of turning away when she noticed a small piece of paper stuck to the glass. It hadn't been there last week.

'Part-time assistant required.
Some evenings and weekends.'

Andi caught her breath. This was it! Exactly what she had been looking for. How she wished Liz was still with her for moral support. She smoothed her hair down and tried to psych herself up to go in and ask.

Then she remembered the present Liz had given her. She slid the portrait card out of the gift bag and looked quickly at her horoscope. It had said something about her being assertive and extrovert. Yes, there it was: . . . ruling planet Jupiter . . . made her ambitious, always projecting her mind towards new horizons . . . but, now she had time to read on, the rest wasn't so positive. In fact, if she believed in astrology, then she shouldn't apply for this job at all. All the portents were against it. Good thing she didn't, she thought to herself and shoved the card back into the bag. She would just forget all that stuff in her chart about taking a fateful step which she might regret.

But . . . why was it that when you tried to put something out of your mind it always came popping to the surface? The last lines which Pam had written kept running through her head.

Employment prospects loom on the horizon. Soon you will have a decision to make. You are right to be apprehensive. Be sure this is what you want. Be careful, things aren't always what they seem.

'Nonsense!' Andi spoke aloud, and pushed open the shop door.

THREE

The shop was completely empty. Andi peered around her. Because of the gloom it was difficult to see into all the corners. She went and stood by the sales counter. There was a basket full of rock crystals which she loved running her fingers through. Polished and unpolished stones: black diamond, jade and jet, tiger's eye and some from the hills around the town, cairngorm and white marble. She liked the feel of them in her hands, their stillness and purity.

She waited for a moment or two and then went over to a rack of skirts and tops and started to look through them. There were some beautiful hooded blouses which hadn't been there the last time she was in. She lifted one out to examine it more closely. It was made of crushed satin in a deep glowing red. It ran through Andi's mind that the horoscope had mentioned something about red. She smiled to herself. One moment she was chivvying Liz for paying too much attention to astrology and the next thing she was allowing her own prediction to influence her choice of clothes. She replaced the blouse, and moved on to the rail with the kaftans. She took

13

down a full-length purple and green one with a high collar. Now that could look quite spectacular, especially with her long blonde hair piled high on her head.

She held the kaftan in front of her and moved over to the mirror. It was almost worth coming into the shop alone just to look at that. It was a tall cheval-glass, framed with the most intricately decorated wood. It stood on its swivel base of great claws fashioned from oak, and at the top it had a huge globe of the moon in dull silver. All around the outside it was carved with fantasy creatures, dragons and trolls, unicorns and mermaids. Every time she visited the shop Andi saw something new among the carvings. She would spot some extra detail that she hadn't noticed before. She reached her hand out to touch a strange bird with a ring held firmly in its beak.

'Can I help you with anything today?' said a voice behind her.

Startled, she twirled round quickly. It was the owner. He had come silently through from the back shop and was standing watching her. Andi couldn't make out his expression behind his glasses, the steel frames seemed to give his face a cold and forbidding appearance.

'Um, no,' she stuttered, 'that is . . .'

'The kaftan,' he said helpfully, indicating the garment she still held in her hand, 'did you want to try it on?'

'Oh, this,' said Andi. 'No, I was just day-dreaming.'

She reached up hurriedly to put it back where she had taken it from. In her haste she missed the rail and the dress fell to the floor. She bent to pick it up and realised her face must now be bright pink. She was making an idiot of herself behaving like this. She couldn't ask for a job now, she decided. Who would want to employ someone who was so clumsy to help out in a shop? She would look around at a few more things and then go. What a wasted opportunity. She was annoyed with herself for being so indecisive. She glanced over at him. He had gone behind the counter and was sorting through some rings, replacing the empty spaces on the ring pad with new ones which he had just brought from the back.

I would love to do something like that, Andi thought suddenly, and I could certainly arrange a more eye-catching display. He didn't have a clue, the way he was shoving them in willy-nilly, with not even the most attractive side facing uppermost.

He saw her looking at the rings. 'Definitely nothing you're interested in?' he asked again. His voice was more friendly this time, less hostile and supicious.

'Yes,' she said, making up her mind swiftly. It was now or never. 'There is. I'm interested in your vacancy for a part-time assistant.' She took a deep breath and waited. He could only say no. There was a long silence.

'Of course,' he said. 'I should have realised . . .' He stopped. 'Yes, indeed, a girl like you . . .'

He paused again. 'You're always interested in the unusual things, I've noticed.'

Andi smiled at him hopefully.

'I'm sorry,' he said.

She felt bitter disappointment flood through her. So silly, she thought, to get all wound up over a small part-time job in a shop.

'I'm sorry,' he continued, 'I have to ask. How old are you?'

'Sixteen,' said Andi in relief. 'Well, almost,' she added truthfully. 'In a few weeks, to be exact.'

'Umm,' he hesitated, 'I do need help for Christmas-time. It's for Saturdays and late-night opening on Fridays, and if you could stay after closing for an hour on a Thursday night to open the new deliveries.

'Oh, yes!' said Andi, eyes glowing.

'Yes, everybody thinks it's very exciting to open the new parcels but it gets boring after a while. I had another girl who worked for a few weeks but she left the other day without giving notice. Just never turned up and didn't even ring me.' He grunted. 'That's teenagers for you.'

'Not all teenagers,' said Andi quickly. 'I'm a very reliable person.'

He almost smiled at her remark. 'I'm sure,' he said.

'And I'm interested in the goods you sell,' she went on. 'I am quite artistic, I could do a terrific window display for Christmas. You might sell more if things were laid out attractively.'

'You mean they're not now?' he asked.

Andi felt her face go red again. 'No . . .' She glanced around her. 'Well, not very,' she said bravely.

To her surprise he laughed out loud. 'At least I don't need to ask if you're honest,' he said.

'I can get references if you like,' said Andi at once.

'Tell you what.' He tore a piece of paper from a notepad beside the till. 'Write your name, address and telephone number down. There have been other people asking besides you. I'll think it over and I'll get in touch.'

Andi scribbled down the details he had asked for. There, she thought as she handed him the slip of paper, that proves that you shouldn't pay any heed to horoscopes or daft predictions.

FOUR

The telephone was ringing as Andi turned the key in her front door. She flung her school bag on to the floor and ran through to the kitchen and picked it up.

'Hello?' She swung her hair back from her face and cradled the telephone receiver against her chin. 'Hello?' she repeated.

There was a silence on the other end of the phone line.

'Hello. Hello,' said Andi cheerfully. 'Anybody there?'

Silence. The kind of waiting silence that lets you know that there *is* someone there.

'Hello?' she repeated once again. 'Hel . . .' Andi hesitated, she thought she'd heard something. A soft indrawn breath. 'Hello. Is that you, Liz?' she asked. She glanced at her watch. Sometimes Liz phoned her during her break at the shoe market.

The silence went on. As if there was no one at the other end of the line. But Andi knew that there was. Could somehow sense that someone was there. Suddenly there was a sharp click and the dialling tone buzzed in her ear. 'Oh, for heaven's sake!' she said and hung the phone back up on the kitchen wall.

Surely she wasn't actually getting freaky phone calls? Not here. Not in her own home, at this time in the early evening. She shook her head, crossed the kitchen floor and pulled open the fridge door. She rummaged through the shelves until she found two pizza bases, then she placed them on the counter and started to look for fillings. The tomato purée was in the top cupboard. Just enough and no more, she thought as she squeezed the tube determinedly. The red liquid oozed out and she spread it across the dough with the flat edge of a chopping knife. Red was supposed to feature in her life according to the prediction. She smiled to herself, perhaps it was coming true after all. Now for the toppings; tomato, ham and pineapple for her. Sliced salami, peppers, onion and mushroom for her dad. She arranged them carefully, sprinkled some shredded mozzarella cheese on top then stepped back to admire her handiwork. She adjusted the red and green pepper slices.

'Creative.' That's what Mr Rodney, the art teacher, had told her dad at the last parents' evening. 'Creative and imaginative, with a definite artistic flair.'

'A bit too imaginative sometimes.' Her dad had teasingly pulled her hair as they walked across the school car park. Andi had laughed. She knew what he meant. She could always make a dramatic scene out of ordinary events. 'Everyday life is too dull for our Andi,' her dad always said.

When she was younger she would make up

stories about people passing in the street, inventing whole new lives for them, usually with terribly sinister backgrounds. Ordinary neighbours with appalling secrets to hide. And just now . . . she shook her head at her own silliness. Becoming alarmed over a simple wrong number. It happened a thousand times a day. She had done the same thing herself on occasion. Dialled the wrong digits, and then hung up at once when she realised her mistake.

Only . . . Andi frowned and her eyes clouded; if she did do that then she would always say *something*, like 'sorry' or 'my mistake'. She smiled at her own thoughts. There she was, off again. Why did she keep doing this? Liz would put it all down to planetary influences, saying it was her astrological destiny. Incredible really, thought Andi, to think that people's lives could be influenced in such a way. She went to the kitchen door, opened it and stood outside on the step for a moment. It was almost completely dark but the night sky was clear. The distant stars glowed in the cold air. The corners of her mouth turned up as she remembered the nursery rhyme from when she was little.

> *Star light, Star bright,*
> *First star I see tonight,*
> *I wish I may, I wish I might,*
> *Have the wish I wish tonight.*

What would she wish for? Some piece of jewellery as a gift for her birthday? Her dad couldn't afford anything too expensive. No, not that then. She closed her eyes. She knew what to wish for.

'I hope I get the job in Moonstone,' she murmured. Some interesting work after school or on a Saturday would give her an income and some independence. And she would enjoy working in that particular shop. She knew she would, despite the fact that the owner seemed a bit strange.

Andi went back into the house and switched on the cooker. She glanced at the clock as she opened the oven door. Nearly half-past five. Her dad would just be leaving the insurance office where he worked in the city. Andi slid the baking tray with the pizzas on to the middle shelf and set the timer. They would be cooked and hot, with the cheese bubbling, in time for him walking in the door. She turned round and caught the blur of her own reflection on the kitchen window.

'Oh!' she gasped, and she was suddenly aware of herself standing there in the light and the darkness outside. 'Dope,' she told herself. But couldn't help the next thought following on. She was vulnerable, alone in the house and quite visible if anyone should be watching her. She stretched out and flicked off the kitchen light. There, she thought, now I'll go through to the living room and watch TV until Dad comes home. She turned to leave the kitchen.

The telephone rang again.

She stared at it for a second and then strode briskly across the kitchen floor and lifted the receiver from the wall. 'Hello. Who is calling, please?'

Silence. Nothing.

But not completely. Echoing faintly along the line she was sure she could hear something. What? Andi's fingers gripped the phone tightly. 'I – ' she began.

Then she recalled the advice they had been given in school guidance classes. Don't let the caller hear any reaction. Hang up quickly and quietly. She reached forward to replace the receiver gently on the wall. As she did, her head turned towards the kitchen window.

At the window there was a face, gleaming white, pressed against the glass.

FIVE

Andi gasped and the phone fell from her fingers. She stepped back quickly, her heart thudding noisily in her chest. The face flattened itself against the mottled glass panel. Distorted and grotesque, it seemed to leer in at her, alone and afraid. Andi couldn't move, couldn't speak. She stood there, unable to cry for help.

Suddenly the face disappeared. One moment it was there, the next it had gone. Andi breathed out slowly. Her hands were shaking. This time it wasn't the workings of her overactive brain. She *hadn't* imagined it. She hadn't. Someone was out there prowling about.

There was a soft rasping sound. Andi's gaze moved slowly round the kitchen to the source of the noise. It was coming from the back door. She heard it again, a quiet grinding. Her eyes dropped down. The handle of the kitchen door was slowly turning. Andi watched it, eyes staring, hypnotised.

Suddenly she remembered something. She had been outside to look at the stars. On her return had she relocked the door? She should have done it automatically, without thinking. But . . . sup-

23

posing she hadn't? She didn't have time now to rush over and turn the key. What could she do?

She looked round her desperately. What was there to defend herself with? She moved quickly back to the worktop and her hand reached out, almost instinctively, seeking the razor-sharp kitchen knife which she had left lying beside the chopping board. Her fingers found the handle and she picked it up, then she brought it slowly round in front of her. The blade was blood-red.

'Ohh.' Andi gage a tiny moan of fear. Then she realised what it was. Globs of tomato purée still clung along its edge. She grasped it firmly and held it in front of her.

She waited . . . staring at the door. Suddenly the handle was released. There was a silence. Andi couldn't take her eyes away from the door. Her fingers tightened. The skin across her knuckles gleamed white. The knob was given another quick turn and an impatient rattle. Then silence. Andi gasped aloud with relief. She *had* relocked the door. What would the person outside do now? She listened. Was that footsteps creeping quietly away or was there still someone standing there? Waiting.

She would telephone her dad, she decided. She glanced at the kitchen clock and bit her lip. He would already have left the office, she wouldn't be able to contact him. How long did he usually take? Half an hour or more in the rush hour. What else could she do? Her neighbours . . . The new ones . . . She would sound like an idiot if she ran next door babbling with fear. She didn't even know if they would be home at this time. There was Mrs Todd across the street. If she left by the front door and made a quick dash . . .

Yes, she decided, there was some security in the streetlights. A fast sprint and she would be safe.

Suddenly the front doorbell rang noisily. She let the knife go and it dropped with a clatter on to the tiled floor. She rushed through the hall and almost tripped over her school rucksack lying at the foot of the stairs.

'It's only me,' she heard her father call out as she began to open the door. 'I forgot my key.'

'Oh, Dad!' She flung her arms round him.

'Well, that's a great welcome,' laughed her father.

'You're early,' Andi accused him.

'Yes, I'd cleared up one case and I didn't want to start a new one so late on in the afternoon, so I awarded myself some time off and came home early. I thought you'd be in the kitchen so I went around the back way first, but it was all in darkness.'

'It was you!' gasped Andi.

'Yes,' said her dad. Then he looked at her more closely. 'Who did you think it was? Is there anything wrong?'

'No, no,' said Andi in relief. 'I heard someone trying the back door and I got a fright. My imagination running away with me again.'

'Andi, you know I don't like you being in the house by yourself, even though you are nearly sixteen. You did look through the spyhole and check that it was me standing there before you began to open the front door?'

'Yeah,' said Andi and nodded her head automatically. But, in fact, she hadn't. She felt completely stupid. Overreacting to a wrong number on the telephone and taking fright when someone tried the back door. She should have simply called out and her dad would have answered.

'Hey, what's that all over the front of your blouse?' her dad asked as he put his briefcase down.

Andi glanced down at herself. Smears of tomato purée were streaked down the front of her white polo shirt. 'Blast!' she said.

Her dad laughed. 'I guess that's dinner is it?' He sniffed the air noisily. 'And I'm willing to bet that it's pizza tonight.' He put his arm round Andi's shoulder. 'Lead the way, kiddo, I'm starving.'

They walked through to the kitchen. Her dad opened the cutlery drawer and began to take out knives and forks. Andi spooned some coffee into two mugs. This was her favourite time of day, when the two of them got a chance to chat and catch up with each other's news. In the mornings everything was always too rushed. She would be drying her hair, he would be throwing things in to his briefcase. Later on at night she would be catching up with her homework, and he always brought cases home to study. But now, over dinner, she would talk about school and he would tell her funny stories about his workmates.

She told him about the job in the shop. He

frowned when she mentioned working on a Thursday evening when the mall was closed.

'Oh, Dad, don't be so overprotective. The owner said that he usually goes home to feed and walk his dog for an hour, and he would leave me the shop keys so that I can lock myself in. Also,' Andi held her hand up quickly before her dad could say anything more, 'he told me there's usually a security guard around at night.'

'All the same,' said her dad, 'I'm not too happy about that. Late Fridays and Saturdays are fine. There's a whole crowd of staff leaving at the same time, and plenty of your friends who live close by. I think I'll pick you up on a Thursday. I don't want you coming home by yourself in the dark.'

'That is, always supposing I actually get the job,' Andi sighed. She felt now as though her whole life depended on it. She had already calculated how much spending money she might have accumulated by Christmas.

'Of course you'll get it,' her dad said confidently. 'Didn't you tell him about the wonderful pizzas that you make?'

They had almost finished dinner when the strident ring of the telephone cut across their conversation. Her dad reached behind his head to answer it. 'Sure, sure,' he said, then he gave Andi the receiver. 'Some guy for you.' He covered the mouthpiece with his hand. 'Sounds like a real weirdo.'

SIX

'Andi,' said a strange husky voice.

Andi felt her jaw tighten. Who was this? Who was trying to frighten her?

'Andi?' The voice spoke again. It was a question now.

Andi suddenly felt angry. She remembered the phone calls earlier. How dare they do this to her! 'Right,' she said briskly, 'that's enough. Who exactly are you, and why are you calling this number?'

There was a silence. Then, 'It's Jack Hamilton.'

'I don't know any Jack Hamilton,' Andi snapped.

Her father stopped on the way to the sink with his dishes and raised an eyebrow.

'I'm the owner of Moonstone in the mall,' said the voice. 'You were in the shop earlier. I'm calling you back about the part-time work.'

'Oh,' said Andi. 'Oh, I'm so sorry. I didn't realise.' She covered the mouthpiece with her hand and spoke to her dad. 'It's OK,' she told him 'It's the shopowner calling me about the job.' Andi spoke into the telephone again. 'I'm sorry I was so abrupt,' she said. 'I – '

'That's fine,' said Mr Hamilton. 'Young girls should be careful about strange calls. In fact I don't want you to answer the telephone at all in the shop, even if I'm not there.'

'You mean I've got the job!' cried Andi. 'That's terrific . . . I mean, thanks very much. When can I start?'

'Tomorrow, if you're free,' said Mr Hamilton. 'You're younger than I really wanted, but we can give it a try for Saturday and see how it goes. I'll see you at ten a.m. sharp.'

Andi hung up the phone and ran and hugged her dad. 'I've got it!' she shouted. 'I've got it! Dad, can I phone Liz and ask her over later? I need some help to decide what I'm going to wear.'

'What's wrong with what you've got on?' asked her dad.

'Dad, don't be boring,' Andi said as she dialled the shoe-market number. She hoped that it wouldn't be the shop manageress who answered. Liz wasn't supposed to take private calls at work, but this was an emergency.

'Great,' Liz spoke quickly. 'I told you your prediction would bring you luck. I'll come over right after work. Actually I tried to phone you earlier but the pay phone here wasn't working properly. I heard you answering but you couldn't hear me. I'll call round right after I finish here.'

So that explained the mysterious calls. As she collected her school bag and went upstairs, Andi shook her head at her own nervousness. What had got into her? Liz had mentioned Pam's prediction. Now that she thought about it Andi realised that was when her nervousness had begun today. She remembered her own apprehensiveness when she had read the poster in the mall, her reluctance to sit for her portrait. And then . . . the slight flicker of unease she had felt when she had looked at her picture and studied her own starscape. Liz believed that it would bring her luck. Then why did she, Andi, think the exact opposite? That this particular horoscope was an ill omen?

'What d'you think?' she asked Liz a few hours later as she pulled a hanger of clothes from her wardrobe. 'The successful career-woman look?' Andi struggled into a navy skirt and jacket which she had worn nearly two years ago when she was fourteen.

'Mmm,' Liz surveyed her critically. 'Don't think so, dear,' she said in an affected accent. 'I do believe one has put on a teensy little bit of weight since one last wore that suit, no?'

'One does happen to have developed a few womanly curves, yes,' said Andi, 'because one does not allow oneself to diet to distraction.'

'So you don't support the walking floor-mop look,' said Liz waving a fashion photo magazine under Andi's nose.

'Nope,' said Andi. She took off her jacket and threw it at Liz.

'Ouch!' said Liz from her position lying

among a heap of discarded items on Andi's bed. 'What else have you got?'

'Not a lot,' grumbled Andi, her head inside her wardrobe. 'That's why I need this job. The clothes situation now requires special funding. The government should declare an emergency and send in troops.'

'I think,' said Liz, sitting up and propping a pillow behind her head, 'that what we need is some power dressing.' She picked up a knitted top and threw it at Andi. 'Try that,' she said.

Andi pulled it on over her head. It had a glittering sequined motif appliquéd on the left shoulder. Liz stretched up and stuffed a few paper tissues under each shoulder.

'A little padding here,' she declared, 'and you too could look like Joan Collins.'

The girls fell about shrieking with laughter.

'How about the Versace PVC effect?' asked Andi. She grabbed a plastic carrier bag and wrapped it round her body. Then she sucked in her cheeks and minced around the room.

'Let me add a little extra something,' said Liz, jumping up and rummaging in her bag of Christmas shopping. She unwrapped two red tree baubles and hung them from Andi's ears.

Andi studied herself in her bedroom mirror. 'Fashion victim,' she declared.

'And now to complete your ensemble,' said Liz, 'the correct choice of footwear is essential. Take advice from an expert.'

'Doc Martens?' queried Andi.

'Too clumpy,' replied Liz.

'Cat boots?' asked Andi.

'Too casual,' said Liz.

'Slingback sandals?'

'Get a life.'

'Black suede high heels?'

'Overdone.'

'Trainers?'

'Underdone.'

'Bare feet?' Andi asked desperately.

There was a knock on Andi's bedroom door. Her dad put his head round the door. 'Hi,' he said. 'It's quite late now so I thought maybe Liz might want to call home for her lift.'

Liz looked at her watch and scrambled up from the floor. 'Gosh, is that the time?' she said. 'I didn't realise it was so late. I'd better go.'

'Oh, well done, Dad,' said Andi sarcastically. 'Very subtle. NOT.'

Her dad grinned at her. 'I'm getting the hot chocolate ready downstairs,' he said. 'It's pretty frosty out there tonight.'

'Hey, Dad,' Andi called out after him. 'Do you think this looks OK to wear for work tomorrow?'

'Looks great to me,' her dad called back as he went downstairs.

'Neither of you are any help at all!' wailed Andi, and she slumped down on to the floor. 'My job starts *tomorrow*, Liz, remember? I need advice, *now*.'

'Don't worry,' said her friend. 'Tell me the look you wish to achieve, and I will transform you immediately.'

'I don't know,' said Andi wearily. 'I want to look sophisticated without being overdressed. Not too young but not too old. Trustworthy, reliable but not a complete dipstick.'

'Is that all?' asked Liz. She suddenly caught sight of the mall gift bag lying beside the chest of drawers. 'When in doubt,' she declared, 'let the stars guide your faltering steps.' She took Andi's astral chart and portrait from its wrapping and pinned it on the bedroom wall. 'There,' she said, 'now you can gaze at it night and day.'

Andi looked at her likeness again. She didn't want to offend Liz, but she had gone off it slightly.

'Sagittarius, the archer,' said Liz. 'Ninth sign. Fire. Now that probably has some significance.'

'For goodness sake,' said Andi. 'What possible significance could that have?'

Later, when she switched her night lamp off and settled down, Andi realised that Pam must have used fluorescent pens for some of her artwork. The zodiac symbols had been highlighted and some parts of her astral chart gave off a luminous eerie light. The last thing Andi saw before she fell asleep was the outline of the arrow, and around it, flickering and glowing in the dark were fiery red and orange flames.

SEVEN

'Come on, Liz.' Andi yanked her friend's arm, as Liz wandered in the direction of the news-agent's. 'I don't want to be late. Not on my first day.'

'I was just going to get a mag and check your stars for you,' said Liz.

'I don't need it,' said Andi. She laughed. 'Pam's prediction will do me for the month ahead.'

She took Liz's arm and steered her away from the paper shop. The weekend newspapers were spread out, face up, along the counter. There was another front-page article on the missing teen-ager. Reading it gave Andi a strange feeling. The girl had been in the mall only last week. Perhaps Andi had seen her, even stood beside her in a shop without realising it. And now she was gone. For ever.

They hadn't yet released details of how she had died. There was a lot of gossip about drugs and pushers. According to the police, drug activity in the town had escalated recently. Officers had been in school talking to classes and groups of pupils, and the school-guidance teachers were trying to get the message across.

'Hi!' Someone pulled her hair sharply. Andi yelped and turned around. It was Paul.

'Heard you've got a job.' He grinned at her. 'Welcome to the working classes.' He winked at Liz. 'Think she'll be able to cope with the Saturday rush?'

'I don't know if Moonstone gets a Saturday rush,' said Liz

'Moonstone?' Paul exclaimed. 'You're working in Moonstone! I thought it was the shoe market. What happened to the girl who was working there before? She always bought her lunch at my counter on a Saturday.'

'The owner, Mr Hamilton, said she didn't turn up one day,' said Andi.

'Funny,' said Paul. 'That's what he told *her* about the previous girl. He's a bit strange, isn't he?'

Andi shrugged. 'He seems OK to me,' she said.

'Brilliant, Paul,' said Liz crossly. 'That's going to give Andi a major boost to begin the day. Any other bright remarks to cheer us up?'

'Sure,' said Paul, 'remember the lunchtime Kookie Kounter snacks are the best around. We do a special Slim-and-Select range to cater for your tastes,' he added.

'Sounds like a sexist remark to me,' said Liz. 'Did that sound sexist to you?' she asked Andi.

'Somebody mention sex?' said a voice behind them.

'No luck, Tony,' said Paul. 'And definitely not wearing that track suit.'

'Gosh, is that obligatory in the sports shop?'

asked Liz. 'I thought my boss was bad enough insisting we wore shoe-market specials, but that . . .'

Tony's track suit was red and green with yellow slashing on the arms and legs.

'Actually I chose it myself,' Tony said huffily. 'It's from their new designer range.'

'Bet you got a big discount,' said Liz. 'Or did they actually pay you to take it away?'

'The best favour you could do them is NOT tell anyone where you bought it,' said Paul.

Andi began to feel sorry for Tony. She stretched up and pulled the peak of Paul's Kookie Kounter cap. 'Gee, I hope I get a baseball cap just like yours to wear,' she said.

Paul grabbed her around the waist. 'You might get more than that,' he joked.

Liz clapped her hands. 'Right, break it up, children,' she said. 'Here comes Sedgely, our favourite security guard, and you know his opinion of horseplay in the mall.'

They all lined up and saluted as Sedgely approached.

'Very funny,' he said. 'Isn't it about time you lot were at work?' He looked at Andi. 'You're starting in Moonstone this morning, aren't you?'

'Not a lot gets past you, Sedgely,' said Paul, 'does it?'

Sedgely glared at him, unsure whether he was being wound up or not. 'I keep my eye on everything that happens here,' he said importantly. 'I have been helping the police with their investigations about that teenage girl they found.'

'What about her?' said Andi.

'I'm not at liberty to say,' said Sedgely. 'I can tell you that they are following a certain line of enquiry.'

Andi shivered slightly. Did the police suspect someone in the mall? A particular shopowner, or one of the staff perhaps?

'He's making most of that up,' said Tony as Sedgely walked away.

'Mmm, don't know,' said Paul. 'I've often thought that the mall would be the perfect place to commit a crime. It's so busy that no one would notice.'

'Well, I know someone who will definitely notice if I am late for work,' said Liz. 'I'm going, and so are you,' she said to Andi. She gave her a push in the direction of Moonstone, and then ran towards the shoe market. Andi hung back. It was quite early in the morning and the mall was fairly quiet. Not many people around yet. Some of the weekend traders had still to open up their booths and barrows. Pam was already in place though. An older man had stopped to talk to her, and she was searching for something amongst the papers and sketches on her table. Perhaps he had left a photograph to be done, thought Andi. A sudden idea struck her. She would have Pam paint her father's picture for Christmas. She smiled to herself. She knew exactly where she would hang it in the hall at home. But she wouldn't have his fortune told. He wouldn't appreciate that. In fact she didn't know if she appreciated her own all that much.

She remembered what had Pam written under one of the headings.

Lifestyle: You hate being hemmed in. Trust your instinct. Being in a closed space will make you uneasy.

The shop certainly was a closed space, she thought, and she did hate being confined. So that was two items which were true. But . . . it also said '*trust your instinct.*' And that of course was the problem. She didn't know what her instinct was.

Andi looked around nervously. She *did* want this job. Well, to be absolutely truthful she had wanted *any* job to begin with. But now, yes, she would like to work in Moonstone. The goods it stocked interested her. She liked their ethnic origins, preferred the hand-finished garments to chain-store and boutique clothing. Was that part of her astral make-up? Why was it that she felt more comfortable with things which were closer to their natural origins, than say Liz, who preferred synthetic stuff and glitzy clothes? And if that was the case then what was holding her back now, making her unsure and nervous about starting work today? She didn't really know. It seemed to Andi that some inner being within her had suddenly been awakened. Some part of her that was alert to danger was telling her to watch out. Although . . . maybe it wasn't specifically concerned with the shop and Mr Hamilton. Perhaps her sixth sense was warning her about something more general.

Andi looked at the big clock above the escalator. It was nearly time for her to start. She dismissed these thoughts from her mind. It really was just as well that she didn't actually believe in horoscopes. She was determined, no matter what, that she would succeed in this job. After all, how could there possibly be anything sinister about working in the local shopping mall?

EIGHT

'It's brilliant. I love it.' Andi finished the last of her yoghurt and tossed the empty carton into the waste bin at the end of their bench. 'It's the greatest job in the world.'

Liz laughed. 'How can you tell so soon?' she asked. 'This is only the third Saturday you've been working.'

'I just can,' said Andi. 'I mean, there's bits I'd rather give a miss. Like cleaning and polishing the big carved mirror. I didn't know that would be such a pain. And refolding all the knitwear at night. But I love arranging the jewellery, and I really enjoy the selling side of it.'

Liz nudged Andi sharply with her elbow. 'Not to mention the rather dishy customers who turn up from time to time.' She nodded at a tall boy with long brown hair who was leaning casually over the railing at the top of the mall escalator.

'Leo?' said Andi. 'He's nothing special.'

'I don't think he holds that opinion about you,' said Liz smugly. 'I've noticed how often he is in and out of this mall, and it's always the same shop that he visits.'

Andi gave Leo another sidelong glance. He *did*

come into the shop a lot, buying little gifts for friends. He always selected something from the Zodiac range of toiletries, one of the soaps, bath essence or perfumed oils. He would usually chat to her first and ask her advice. He never took anything from the same sign twice. Either he changed girlfriends every other day or he had a dozen different ones. What was he doing here now? Andi watched him as he leaned over the escalator to see down to the bottom level. The cloth tapestries of the Twelve Days of Christmas were being hung in sequence around the circular railing. Maybe, like her, he enjoyed looking at the Christmas decorations, or perhaps he was waiting for someone. Andi craned her neck forward.

'I'll trade you places, if you want,' said Liz. She inspected the inside of her own sandwich and then bit into it enthusiastically. 'That boss of mine was in an all-time crazy mood this morning. We didn't meet our sales targets for November and she is freaking completely.' Liz started to imitate the shoe-market manageress. 'Only four weeks to Christmas. If things don't improve there'll be no Santa Claus for any of you!' She slurped her milk shake noisily. 'Cruella de Vil in person,' she said. 'Even your Mr Hamilton doesn't take flakies like that.'

'Jack's fine. He just needs a bit of getting used to,' said Andi. Everyone, including her dad, thought Jack Hamilton very dour. At first Andi had found it difficult working with him in the shop, but her natural cheerfulness had always managed to overcome his abruptness. She found that he left her to do more and more on her own initiative. 'He is anxious about the shop,' said Andi. 'The rates are very high, so he has to work quite hard to break even.'

'Well, you'd think he would be a bit more welcoming to customers then,' said Liz.

'I suppose so,' said Andi. She had to admit he could be a bit odd at times. His insistence that she must never answer the telephone. The way he always had to return home at six p.m. every night. To feed and walk his dog, he said. It meant that she was on her own for nearly an hour on late-opening Friday. And also on Thursday, the day she worked extra to sort the new stock. Her dad still wasn't too happy about the fact that she was working there when the mall was closed up on stock day, even though there was a security guard and the night-shift cleaners came in later. He always came to collect her on Thursdays.

'Jack's OK,' said Andi. 'He's not good at relating to people, that's all.'

'What star sign is he?' asked Liz. 'Perhaps it's all to do with his ascending planet.'

'Rubbish!' said Andi. She thought for a minute. 'I think he worries about things, and bottles it all up inside.'

'There you go again,' said Liz, 'with your great imagination. You think he's got a hidden secret.'

'No, I don't,' protested Andi. But, now that Liz had actually said it aloud, perhaps that *was* the explanation for Jack's manner. Maybe he had some personal problem. He did act for most of the time as though he was preoccupied with something else.

Liz stood up. 'I'd better get back,' she said. 'The boss lady told me when I left the shop that twenty minutes was long enough for a Saturday lunch break.' She drank down the last of her milk shake. 'You coming?' she asked Andi.

Andi shook her head. 'I'll wait for a bit longer,' she said.

'It wouldn't by any chance be because Paul, our Kookie Kounter hotshot, gets his lunch about now?' said Liz.

'No, it wouldn't,' replied Andi firmly.

Paul did take his break about this time and he quite often joined the two girls, but Andi wasn't sure if he was really her type. What exactly *was* her type she had yet to work out, but certainly one or two possibilities had appeared over the last week or so. Working in the shop had meant that she had met so many more people. It was one of the things that Andi liked so much about her job, and one of the reasons that she sat out in the mall walkway during her lunch. She loved watching all the shoppers passing to and fro with their packages, imagining what they had in their bags, what presents they had bought and who for. And the stallholders fascinated her too. The man who sculpted the coloured glass animals, working intently with his blowtorch. The girl who sold the ribbons and hair-bands from her barrow. They were very busy and getting busier as it got closer to Christmas. Yet Pam . . . Andi frowned as she watched her. She never seemed to get customers. People frequently stopped beside her, and she handed out little flyers but not many actually sat down to be sketched or have their predictions cast.

Pam didn't really encourage them, Andi thought. She remembered the night Liz and she had stopped to look at her work. Pam hadn't been at all relaxed. She was still acting the same way. If anybody hesitated or lingered at her poster she raised her head and asked them outright if they wanted something special. Andi had discovered that a better technique for selling in the shop was to chat with people for a bit, then quite often they purchased something. Maybe she would stop on her way back from lunch and speak to Pam, then she could ask how work on her dad's portrait was progressing. Suddenly, as if she was aware that someone was studying her, Pam looked up in Andi's direction. A small flicker of annoyance showed on her face, then she gave a brief smile to acknowledge Andi's wave.

Andi looked past her. She could still see Leo hovering to one side. Her heart quickened. Perhaps Liz was right and he did hang about so that she would be there to serve him. She thought he was very cute. But then quite a few customers asked for her by name now. She had got to know their likes and dislikes and what they were looking for in the way of Christmas presents. There were one or two now who dropped in regularly.

She brushed the crumbs from her fringed skirt and picked up her shawl. It was patterned with coloured birds and scroll designs. Jack gave her a huge discount on any clothes that she bought from him. He said she was a great advert for the shop wearing them around the mall. Andi got up and put the shawl across her shoulders. All of a sudden she felt cold. She shuddered. There must have been a freak draught blowing down from the glass panels above her.

She would give Pam a miss today, she decided. A well-dressed business type had stopped beside her easel and she was engrossed in a deep conversation with him. She would just go straight back and start work. She drew the shawl closer round her body.

One pair of eyes followed Andi's movements carefully as she retraced her steps. Watched her closely as she emptied the remains of her lunch into the waste bins, and then started out across the mall. Flat and expressionless, they stared after her coldly as she returned to the shop in the corner.

NINE

As the days passed and Christmas grew closer Andi found that she looked forward more and more to her work in the shop. The days were sharp and cold, and the shops were full of exciting gift ideas and colourful party clothes. Despite what Liz's manager said, the mall was very busy and although most of her friends moaned about their work, Andi found that hers was not at all boring. Leo came in often. Mostly he hung around without saying much but she had found out he was a second-year student at the local college. Jack certainly took a bit of getting used to. He had a difficult manner, very distant and abstracted. He still didn't allow her to deal with telephone calls yet seemed quite willing to let her have a free hand with stock display.

The first Saturday in December Andi had just started her Christmas window when she noticed a group of people coming off the escalator.

'The police are in the mall,' she called out to Jack. She stopped, staple gun in hand, from where she had been pinning the last end of a purple-coloured Indian cotton bedspread to the back of the shop window.

'What?' Jack Hamilton dropped the sheaf of invoices he held in his hand and hurried to the shop door. 'Where?' he asked.

'Two of them got off the escalator a moment ago,' said Andi. 'They're with Sedgely, the security guard. Probably caught somebody filching in one of the shops.'

'Probably,' said Mr Hamilton. 'It does happen more often at this time of year.' He bent down and gathered up his papers. 'I mean, what else could it be?' he added anxiously.

'Might have something to do with that girl who was found in the woods,' said Andi. 'Liz told me they questioned everybody when they found out this was the last place she had been seen.'

'Yes, but that was some time ago. Why are they back now?'

'Dunno.' Andi clambered out of the window. 'But I'll go and find out,' she offered. 'I can ask Pam. Sitting by the escalator she sees everything that's going on.' Andi stood back and eyed the window critically. 'I want to check how this looks from outside anyway.'

'It looks pretty good to me,' said Jack Hamilton.

Andi smiled at him. She liked it when he mentioned that he was pleased with her work. She knew that he appreciated the changes she had made. The shop was much brighter, more attractive, and they were certainly doing more business, but he rarely actually said anything to her about it. She pulled open the door and collided with someone on their way in. It was Leo.

'Oh,' he said. 'Are you leaving?'

Was there disappointment in his voice? Andi wasn't sure.

'Just for a second,' she said, 'to see how the window looks. In fact,' she grabbed his arm, 'you can be of some use. Come and give me your critical appraisal.' She led him into the mall and stood him in front of the window. He looked at it for a minute or two.

'Seems OK,' he said.

'OK! OK?' Andi pretended to be outraged. 'I was hoping for a lot more than a mere OK.'

Leo laughed down at her, and for the first time Andi noticed his eyes. They were blue, a clear bright blue, and his whole face came alive when he smiled. 'Stupendous,' he said. 'Absolutely stupendous and . . . strikingly attractive.'

'That's better,' said Andi.

'And the window's quite nice too,' Leo added softly.

Andi's eyes locked with his for the briefest moment and she stepped back. Leo smiled again at her and then turned to look at the window display. Andi was now in complete confusion. What had happened there? Nothing really, she supposed. Yet . . . something had passed between them. Was this what Liz meant when she said that there were forces at work over which humans had little control? Planets and stars moving above you determining your destiny?

'I assume you're going to add some more goods,' said Leo.

'Yes,' said Andi, her heart jumping again as he

looked at her. 'The spread is the backdrop. I thought I'd have everything in this window gold-coloured. We have a little table of beaten brass in the back shop and I thought I'd bring it out and arrange some copper bangles and necklaces on it. Jack has some fancy gold-embroidered waistcoats due in, and the deep purple cloth draped behind will give it a luxurious look, don't you think?'

'Sounds like a lot of work,' said Leo, 'you'll never get it done today.'

'No,' said Andi. 'I'll finish it next Thursday. I'll have more time to work on it when the shop is closed and we should have our Christmas deliveries by then.'

'So, you'll be working next Thursday?' Leo asked casually.

Andi nodded.

'I might see you then.' He touched her shoulder gently and moved away. She watched him mingle with the rest of the shoppers, and then she noticed Sedgely and the two policemen amongst the crowds. What were they doing? Pam might know. Andi drifted over towards her stall.

'I've no idea what they're up to,' said Pam when Andi asked her. 'People who snoop about like that drive me crazy.'

'Well . . .' said Andi slowly, 'I suppose it is their job.'

'And why are you not at yours?' asked a voice. It was Tony, out from the sports shop to distribute flyers to passers-by. 'I could dump all two hundred of these in the nearest bin,' he said, 'but I'd probably get caught.'

'There's no hiding place when you're in that luminous track suit,' laughed Andi.

Tony stuffed a couple of dozen leaflets into Andi's hands. Then he too saw the policemen. 'Here comes our Christmas *Crimewatch* service,' he said. 'So I'd better not drop this litter all over the mall.' He waved at Sedgely. 'Have a brochure,' he said. 'Special offer for dumb-bells,' Tony paused for a second, 'and weights,' he added. 'To build up your pectorals.'

Sedgely gave him a hard stare. 'I've got my eye on you,' he said. 'If I find bundles of those lying about I'll know where they came from.'

'It's good to know the mall is in safe hands, Sedgely,' said Tony innocently. 'We can all be reassured that your vigilance will protect us.' He turned to the two policemen. 'Any news on that girl's death?' he asked.

'We might be moving on that case very soon,' said the younger officer.

The older constable placed his hand on the other's arm. 'Best not to discuss that here,' he said.

They moved on and Tony walked Andi back to the shop. 'How's your Christmas shopping going?' he asked her.

'Oh, I've a few things still to get.' As she spoke Andi suddenly remembered the photograph she had left with Pam. She had meant to ask her how it was progressing. 'Pam's doing a picture of my dad,' she told Tony. 'I think she could do with the business. She doesn't get a lot of custom and if she's a student then she's going to be really broke.'

'I don't think she's a student,' Tony said, 'and she's certainly not broke. That's designer gear she's wearing. She's a sharp dresser. Not as good as my own label though,' he added with a grin.

Andi climbed back into the window. Jack had brought out the little table and had spent some time polishing it. It glowed with a deep burnished patina. Andi placed it in position. She had been right to use it as the central focal point of the window. Your eye was drawn to it immediately.

'I'll sort out the rest of this next week,' she said to Jack as they were closing up. 'I want to wait for the Christmas deliveries. There's bound to be some good selling lines coming in.'

Andi pulled on her jacket. She was almost sorry to go home today. She was looking forward to next Thursday evening; she would be able to finish dressing the window, and Leo had hinted that he would drop by.

'Leo,' Liz had told Andi, 'that's a fire sign, same as you, Sagittarius. Like to like, so you are suited. But he could be domineering and bossy and you don't want him to have the upper hand. So be warned. There are parts of his nature that are dangerous for you . . .'

TEN

The next Thursday, as soon as she heard the first announcement for the shops closing, Andi went to the doorway of Moonstone and looked out into the mall. She was desperate to start work on her window. The parcels had arrived and were stacked in the storeroom. She could hardly wait to bring them through and begin opening them. The lights in the other shops were starting to go off now. Andi watched the throng of people in the main walkway. She could hear the rattle of the chain-link security shutters as they were pulled down. Some shoppers were still going into shops for last-minute items but most of the people passing her were struggling with their parcels and bags towards the exits. There was a bustling excitement in the air. Andi hugged herself. She loved the weeks before Christmas. Everyone else always moaned that it started earlier each year, but it couldn't begin soon enough for her. The coloured streetlights and bright decorations thrilled her; she loved keeping secrets from friends and family, and the extended shopping trips to find just the right gift. It was almost better than the actual day itself.

Andi heard the second Tannoy message announcing that the mall would close in fifteen minutes. The shoppers near her began looking at their watches. She looked at hers. 'Better cash up the till,' she muttered to herself.

She turned back into the shop and gave a quick glance around. There were no customers there. She didn't often get tail-enders. The last-minute shoppers in the mall usually headed towards the food outlets. She smiled. Paul would be rushed off his feet at the Kookie Kounter. There was always a staff bonus if the stock in the glass display cases was cleared before closing time. Paul was the Kookie Kounter's top sales assistant. There were never any leftovers at his side of the counter.

Andi could just picture him at this moment. With his dark eyes sparkling and his baseball cap pushed back on his head, he would give a cheeky grin as he went into his closing-time sales pitch. 'Hi, happy shoppers!' he'd be calling to passers-by. 'Best late-night bargain in the mall. These cookies normally retail at twenty-five pence each. I'm giving them away tonight at four for a pound. Hurry! Hurry! Hurry!' Then he'd wink at some good-looking girl and add under his breath, 'Hey, darling. You can have two for fifty pence if you swear not to tell anyone else.'

Andi went through to the office at the back of the shop. She felt quite flattered that Mr Hamilton trusted her enough to do the cashing-up at night. The office was empty. He must be in the stockroom, she thought, as she leaned across the desk and opened the top drawer. She picked up the cash-register keys, and as she did so the telephone just beside her rang. Andi pushed the drawer closed as the phone rang again. Without thinking she reached over and picked up the receiver as the bell sounded the third time. 'Hello, Moonstone. Can I help you?'

There was a silence and then a strange whimpering sound came echoing down the line. 'No, no,' said a weak voice, a woman's voice, 'not another girl.'

'I'm sorry,' said Andi. 'I can't hear you properly. Can you speak up?'

'You're a girl, aren't you?' The voice seemed a little stronger now.

'Well, yes, last time I looked,' Andi joked.

'Oh, no,' the woman whispered. Her voice trembled as she went on. 'I told him. I begged him. Not another one.'

'I don't know what you mean,' said Andi. The person on the other end of the phone sounded terribly upset, almost as if she was too frightened to speak. 'Have you got the correct number?' said Andi.

'I think so,' came the reply. 'You're in Moonstone, the shop in the mall, working for Jack Hamilton?'

'That's it,' said Andi. 'You've got the right place.'

'Yes, yes, I thought so,' said the woman urgently. 'As you say, I've got the right place. It's *you* that's in the wrong place, and you must leave at once.'

'Leave?' Andi repeated. 'Why should I leave?'

'Because – '

'Who are you talking to? What are they saying?' There was a loud shout behind Andi. She turned quickly as Mr Hamilton came from the stockroom. He crossed the floor and snatched at the telephone wire. With a sudden abrupt gesture he ripped the flex out from the wall. 'I told you not to answer the phone, didn't I?' He slammed his fist on the desk. 'Didn't I?' he repeated angrily.

Andi jumped back nervously. 'Well, yes,' she said. 'I'm sorry, I just picked it up automatically. I was at the desk collecting the till keys.' She looked at them still clasped in her fingers. Her hands were shaking. 'I think I'll go and cash up now.' She walked past him into the front shop. At the counter she turned the key in the till, entered the code, and pressed the button. The machine started to print out the day's transactions.

Andi's mind was churning almost as fast as the paper roll was spilling out in front of her. Who had called the shop? Why had she been so startled to discover that there was a female assistant? What was wrong with Andi being a girl? Why was the caller so anxious? 'Not another girl,' the voice had said. A woman's voice. A voice filled with fear.

Andi tore off the day's end statement from the machine and started to put the takings into the cash bag. She was trembling a little. She bit her lip and leaned on the counter to steady herself. Perhaps she would just give up this job. She didn't want to work for someone who lost his temper so easily and shouted at her. And she knew that her dad wouldn't want her to be somewhere that she wasn't happy.

But, she *did* like serving in the shop. There were so many different types of customers to deal with and often they asked her advice. It made her work interesting. She would have hated being at a supermarket checkout all day. Mr Hamilton gave her a lot of freedom in organising the goods. She made most of the decisions about stock layout. She enjoyed sorting out the earrings, necklaces and belts and making up the displays. Of course Liz told her that this was all to do with her star sign, that she was developing her inner powers and becoming more creative. But Andi had also found that she had got used to Mr Hamilton. He was a bit surly but she found that if she chatted away he would nod and smile occasionally.

And yet . . . there was the telephone call. Why was she not supposed to answer the phone? Why had he been so angry when she had? Someone had tried to tell her something. To warn her. About what?

A faint rustle sounded just behind her. Andi turned around and gasped. She was not alone. There was someone else in the shop. Standing beside the long Indian silk scarves was a tall dark figure, watching her.

ELEVEN

The figure moved towards her.

'Leo!' Andi gasped. 'I didn't notice you coming in.'

'Sorry if I gave you a fright,' said Leo. 'I came in . . . for . . . to buy . . .' He looked round him vaguely. Then he caught sight of the collection of long Indian silk scarves. 'A scarf,' he said. He pulled one out from its peg. 'What d'you think of this one?' he asked. It was a beautiful muted blue with twists of grey and silver throughout.

'It's lovely,' said Andi. 'Who is it for?'

'Emm . . .' Leo hesitated. 'Well, me, I think.'

Andi watched him as he fingered the silky folds. He seemed very unsure of himself, as if he had just made up a reason to be in the shop. He placed the scarf beside his face.

'I mean, I thought I could tie my hair back in a bandana with it. Do you think I would suit that?'

Andi put her head on one side and studied him for a moment. 'Could look terrific,' she said. 'It would pick up the blue in your eyes. Tell you what. Why don't you try it on, while I clear this away.' She picked up the cash bag. 'Back in a moment,' she said, and smiled at him. In the office Mr Hamilton was sitting at the desk with his head in his hands. He looked up quickly as Andi came in.

'Look,' he said, 'I'm sorry that happened. I didn't mean to shout at you. It's just that ... Well, I thought that the caller was frightening you and that's why I rushed over. We have had strange phone calls here in the past.' He paused. 'I will understand if you don't want to stay on to do the window tonight.'

Andi suddenly felt sorry for him. He seemed so dejected. She had reacted too hastily. He had only been trying to protect her. 'I'll wait,' she said, handing him the cash bag, 'until you get back from walking the dog at any rate.'

I can stay on for an hour at least, Andi thought to herself. He *has* apologised, and she didn't really want to miss going over the new stock. It was one of her favourite jobs.

'There's one last customer out there,' she said. 'I'll attend to him and then I'll get the keys from you and sort out the stock.' She went back to the front shop. Leo was standing before the carved cheval mirror. He had the scarf bunched over his hair and scrunched up at the back.

'What a mess!' laughed Andi. 'Here let me.' She had to stretch right up to reach the top of his head. She adjusted the scarf carefully, smoothing it out so that the pattern could be seen.

'I'm too tall for you,' Leo said, and he leaned down so that Andi could retie the knot. For a brief moment their faces touched, and Andi caught his gaze. He was staring at her. The light bright blue of his eyes was intense. Andi stepped back, feeling suddenly awkward.

'You're very pretty,' Leo said softly. 'Do you have lots of boyfriends?'

Andi blushed. 'Dozens,' she joked quickly. She turned away. 'Check out your reflection,' she went on, changing the subject, 'and tell me what you think.'

Leo looked at himself in the mirror. 'Great,' he said. 'I'll buy it.'

'Let me wrap it up for you.' Andi held out her hand to take the scarf back.

Leo struggled with the knot for a moment or two. 'Looks like I'm going to have to wear it,' he said. 'I can't undo it.'

'Silk is a very strong fabric,' said Andi ringing up the sale, 'but if you take it off I'll unpick the knot.'

'I see what you mean,' said Leo. He took off the scarf and wound the ends around each hand and pulled the material taut. 'It's pretty tough.' He wound it around his neck and made choking noises.

'Gross!' said Andi. 'Hand it over here.' She spread out some tissue paper and, laying the scarf flat on the counter, she folded it carefully. 'I think that's the last one with this particular pattern,' she commented as she wrapped it up.

'Will you be working very late tonight?' Leo asked her.

Andi shook her head as she stuck sellotape on the package. 'Just for an hour. To sort out today's deliveries and finish the window.'

'The deliveries?' Leo repeated and he looked around.

'In the stockroom,' explained Andi. 'It's one of my favourite tasks in the shop. Maybe we'll have some more of those zodiac bath oils and soaps for you next week.' She handed him his purchase. 'Meanwhile, here's your scarf.'

'Every time I wear it I'll think of you,' said Leo. 'And if I need the knot done up properly I know where to come.'

'All part of our after-sales service,' said Andi cheerfully. She followed him to the door and watched him as he walked away. Despite what she had told Liz earlier she was beginning to think he *was* rather special. She saw him stop to speak to Pam. Then he stepped on the down escalator.

Pam was sketching furiously at her easel. Her hands moved back and forth across the cartridge paper with an almost frenetic nervous energy. Andi watched her as she turned to her box of crayons, scrabbling impatiently amongst them to find the right colour. There was no sitter on the little canvas stool. Probably working on her photograph commissions, Andi thought, and remembered again the one of her dad which she had given to Pam. She could take the opportunity now and ask how it was progressing.

'Hi!' she called out, and waved.

Pam looked up and frowned. Then she gave a little wave back. As Andi came over she jumped quickly to her feet and began to bundle everything on the table into her holdall.

'Hey, what's the big rush?' asked Andi. She glanced at the outline portrait on the easel just as Pam threw a cloth over it. The picture was a mass of scrawls and scribbles in lurid colours. 'Gosh,' Andi couldn't help the next words coming out, 'that's weird.'

'Do you mind?' snapped Pam.

'No offence,' said Andi. 'It's just not like anything I've seen you draw before.' She indicated Pam's sample board which was attached to the ornamental railings. Then she remembered why she had come over. 'Done any work on my dad's picture yet?' asked Andi.

'No,' said Pam abruptly.

Andi had already started to sift among the stuff on Pam's table to see if she could find the sketch. Her hand brushed a box of charcoal on to the tiled floor. It burst open and small pieces of paper with names and numbers on them scattered on the ground.

'Sorry,' said Andi. 'I've messed up all your order slips.' She bent to pick them up.

'I'll get them' said Pam quickly. She gathered them up hurriedly and stuffed them into the pocket of her jeans. Then she began to quickly sweep all the rest of the material from her table into her bag.

'Are you all right?' asked Andi. 'You seem a bit tense tonight.'

Pam licked her lips nervously and flicked her hair out of her eyes. 'It's that guy, what's-his-name, Leo. He gives me the creeps, always hanging round here.'

'Leo?' exclaimed Andi. 'He's OK.' Andi looked after him. She could see him getting off the escalator near the fountain. The café downstairs was closing. He walked past it towards the door of the underground car park.

'Well, I don't think he's OK,' said Pam, and her hands shook as she fastened the straps of her bag. 'I don't think he's OK at all. In fact,' she added, 'I think there's something really peculiar about him.'

TWELVE

'Peculiar!' Andi repeated in surprise. 'You're talking about Leo?'

'Yes, him!' said Pam. 'He's always wandering around here, peering over my shoulder, wandering into your shop, then out again. He's definitely odd.'

'Do you think so?' Andi frowned a little. Then she laughed. 'I was just thinking a moment ago that I kind of liked him.' Had she fallen for the old tradition of the tall, good-looking guy? Andi wondered. No . . . there must be something else that had attracted her, but what?

'Huh!' said Pam. Her voice was sharp and strained. 'What's there to like? No conversation. No talent. I think he's creepy.'

Andi looked behind Pam's head. She leaned closer to her. 'If you want to see someone that's mega-creepy then take a look behind you.'

Pam swung her holdall on to her shoulder and turned round. Sedgely was walking towards them.

'Evening, ladies.' He nodded to the girls. 'Anyone working late tonight?'

'I am,' said Andi. 'And I'm locking the shop

door.' She winked at Pam and added under her breath, 'From the inside.'

'You're safe in my hands, my dear,' Mr Sedgely said. 'I patrol these floors carefully. Nothing escapes my attention.'

'That's what frightens us the most,' Andi whispered to Pam.

'You'll be unpacking those parcels I delivered earlier,' Mr Sedgely went on. 'I helped Jack bring them up from the loading bay. He seemed to have more than usual this week.'

'That will be the Christmas goods,' said Andi. 'I'm going to open them right now. I'm dying to see what's arrived. We have some real neat stuff due in,' she went on enthusiastically. 'I'm dressing the window for Christmas in purple and gold.'

'Talking of deliveries,' interrupted Pam. 'I was due a box today, but there was nothing there when I looked downstairs.'

'Well, the bay has been cleared,' said Mr Sedgely. 'If it did arrive perhaps it got mixed up with another order.'

'What!' said Pam sharply. 'It better not be!' She stopped. 'I mean . . . I don't see how it could. It would be clearly addressed.'

'Not everyone is as efficient as I am, dear,' said Mr Sedgely patronisingly. 'Don't worry, we'll check tomorrow with all the shops I delivered to today.'

'Let's check now,' said Pam angrily. 'You must have a list in your office. At least if I look at that I may have an idea who has my stuff.' She stamped off towards the stairs.

Mr Sedgely made a face at Andi and followed her. Andi felt quite sorry for him as she watched him trail after Pam. Pam seemed in a real rage about her parcel going astray. It could only be artist materials and the mall was closed for business for the day, so what could one night's difference possibly make? In fact Pam seemed generally upset about everything tonight. Crotchety and critical of poor Leo. Still, who could blame her if business was poor?

Andi smiled to herself. Maybe it was due to Pam's star sign. Aries, tempestuous and impatient. Did the fact that she had been born at a certain time make her more liable to behave in a particular way? Should you be mindful of warnings and alter your life accordingly? Andi had always been sceptical of people who did. But perhaps it was helpful to be made aware of certain pitfalls, then you could watch out more carefully to avoid them.

Watch out . . . Be careful . . .

But if she believed in horoscopes then she, Andi, wouldn't have taken the job in the mall. Everything had warned against it. She was glad now that she didn't let predictions run her life. She turned and caught sight of Mr Hamilton waiting for her in the shop doorway.

'Sorry,' she said breathlessly as she hurried over. 'I didn't realise that I was holding you back.'

He grunted in reply and gave her the keys. 'I'll just wait while you lock the shutter from the inside,' he said. 'I'll be about an hour and I'll knock on the window on my return.'

Andi took the keys from him.

'You're a good girl, Andi,' he said suddenly. 'I'd be sorry to lose you.'

Andi blushed and, lowering her head, she quickly ducked under and pulled down the shutter. He gave her a brief nod and then stalked off towards the stairs. Poor wee dog, Andi thought, waiting for someone like that to take you for a walk. I'll bet he never talks to it. She had asked Jack once what it was called and he had just shrugged. Imagine not even giving it a pet name. He hadn't seemed to know what breed it was either.

In the stockroom she picked up the smallest parcel and took it out to the front counter. It had some writing on it but the ink had run and the label was blotched. It had 'FRAGILE' marked on it, and some other words: 'STRICTLY' and then the rest was blurred, she could only make out what looked like an 'L'. She began to unwrap the box carefully. The stuff was double wrapped in lots of little packets. One had burst open and the powder had spilt out. Bath salts, thought Andi. It must be more of the toiletry range which Leo liked to buy. He had bought so many different ones over the last few days. Perhaps she was developing a great sales technique. Then she recalled what Pam had said about his being creepy. Well, she didn't think he was creepy, but . . . he *did* hang about the shop a lot. Now that she came to think of it, he had said he was buying them for his girlfriend yet had bought items for three different signs.

Andi's hand stopped in mid-air as she remembered. A bath oil for Aries, then the Gemini shampoo and a . . . what was the latest one? Oh yes, a fish-shaped soap. Which would mean that his girlfriend was a Pisces. She couldn't be all three. The three separate signs meant presents for three girls. Had Leo lots of different girlfriends? He didn't look as though he was the shallow type. Not like Paul, Andi thought with a smile, he had about ten girls on a string promising undying love to all of them. Though that was slightly different, she decided. They all knew about each other. It was a huge game with all of them. But Leo wasn't Paul. Wasn't at all like him in fact. Andi shivered slightly in the cool storeroom. Could Pam possibly be right after all? Was Leo a bit strange?

In the basement level of the mall Leo's car had stopped at the exit barrier.

'Terrible weather,' said the car-park attendant. He nodded at the sleeting rain outside as he handed Leo his ticket and took his money.

'Mmm,' said Leo, holding out his hand for his change. He studied the voucher he had been given which had the date and time of his leaving the underground parking. Then he tucked it carefully in his pocket. 'Oh look!' He held out one of the coins in his hand. 'You've given me a foreign coin.'

The attendant took it back and looked at it. 'No, it's not,' he said. 'That one's straight up.'

'Sorry,' said Leo, taking it back. 'It must be the light.'

'Need your eyes tested,' came the muttered reply as the red and white pole went up.

Leo let out the clutch and his car slid forward. The road outside was jammed with vehicles. Leo pulled into line. The traffic lights at the junction were at red. The rain was slashing down now. He switched the wipers on, and as the windscreen cleared he could see the mall entrance ahead. The main gate was closed over, and the fluorescent signs were going out one by one.

Leo looked up to where the Moonstone shop lights still shone out from the darkness. His eyes, usually a pale cool blue, had a sparkle in them. There was an empty space by the side of the road. Leo hesitated for a second, then he smiled and drew quickly into the empty space. He got out and locked the door. He glanced around him and pulled up the hood of his duffel jacket.

Then, with long determined strides, he began to walk back the way he had come.

THIRTEEN

Andi took out some more of the bath salts and laid them on the counter. She rummaged around in the box to try and locate the invoice, pulling out some small packets. Then she gave up. She decided she wasn't taking up any more of her time doing this. She would leave this lot here for Jack to see to and go back to the stockroom. What she really wanted to do was to find the gold-embroidered waistcoats and see if any other accessories had arrived which would be suitable for her window. She glanced towards where the purple bedspread was draped like an elegant hanging in a royal palace. When she reset the spotlights it would be a perfect foil for the rest of the display.

A half-shadow flitted in the corner of her vision. Puzzled, Andi looked back again to the window, and then smiled at herself. It was a shop sign flickering, that was all.

She picked up a marker pen from beside the till and went through to the back of the shop. The stockroom was very quiet. It was so small that there was scarcely room for her to work. She rubbed the back of her neck. She was certainly uncomfortably hemmed in now. Right, she told herself firmly, get to work, that will concentrate the mind.

She hummed quietly to herself as she ripped open the parcels. She moved a large cardboard box to one side and picked up a showcard and the chunky felt marker. She would write out some prices and do some fancy outlines so that they would be ready for her to place in the display. Mr Hamilton had told her that he preferred her calligraphy to some of the commercially printed notices. In fact, it occurred to her as she began to write, that he relied on her judgement in quite a few things now. He must trust her. Probably that's what he'd been trying to say when he had spoken to her so gruffly as he was leaving earlier.

The cardboard box wobbled as she leant on it. Andi tutted. There was something stuck under the edge. She moved the box to one side and picked it up. It was a crumpled newspaper. Mr Hamilton must have been reading it. She smoothed it out. It seemed an odd thing to do. To crush it up and throw it on the floor. People normally folded a newspaper when they finished reading it. Unless of course they were in a temper about something they had read ... She picked up the newspaper. Why had Mr Hamilton shoved it under the box? Almost as though he was hiding it. Was there something in it that he didn't want her to see?

She smoothed it out carefully and read the headline: 'MISSING IN THE MALL'. Another missing person. Her eyes scanned the page quickly. A girl, about her age . . . she had disappeared on her way home from work a few weeks ago. She had worked – Andi's eyes widened – in . . . Moonstone.

Andi sat back on her heels. Was there a link? It was the second girl to go missing in a short period of time, both with a connection to the mall. Had Mr Hamilton put the paper away to prevent her seeing it? Andi leant over the page again to read the details.

With her head bent, and her long hair hanging on each side of her face, Andi didn't hear the first soft movement behind her. It was only when the sound came again, very faintly, that she raised her head. What was that? She looked round. A pile of leather belts lay on the floor. The buckles must have knocked together as they slid to one side. She looked at them carefully. They hadn't moved.

The noise again, a dull chink. It was equally faint but lasted longer so now she could tell that it was from somewhere behind her. It was coming through the office from the shop. What made a sound like that? There was no fan or air-conditioning unit switched on.

She held her breath and then, just as she was breathing out slowly, she heard it once more. A grating noise, clack, clack, clack. Then silence. The silence continued, on and on, as Andi sat motionless, head on one side, listening.

She waited. Then . . . this time, quite distinctly, she heard the rattle of gridded metal. Andi's hand jerked with fright and the newspaper fell from her fingers. The noise she had just heard was the sound of someone stealthily raising the shop's security shutter.

She stood up quickly. Apart from her, no one else should have a shop key. She stepped through to the office. The keys were lying on the desk beside the telephone. She always supposed Mr Hamilton had another set but they had an agreed procedure for when he returned at night. He always knocked on the outside window. Then she would walk through to the front shop so that she could see who was there before opening up.

Usually when she was working in the front shop she saw the security guard on duty doing his rounds, but they didn't carry the spare sets of keys on them. They were kept in the main office downstairs in case one of the alarms went off. Sedgely always gave her a wave at least. Despite their patrols, Andi always felt safer with the shutter securely locked from her side.

And she *had* locked it tonight. She knew she had. Mr Hamilton always waited until she had done that before going away to feed his dog. Andi suddenly thought about the dog. She didn't recall him ever buying any dog food, and he didn't know anything about his dog, never talked about it. Usually pet owners had lots of little stories to tell about their animals' antics. He never did. There was something not right about his story, about his reason for returning home each night at the same time. If it wasn't to feed and walk the dog then what could it be? Why did he have to leave the shop at the exact same time each evening? What could he possibly be doing?

Andi raised her head. The door through to the front shop was lying ajar. She had switched the shop lights off to save electricity but some light from the office spilled through. She could see the outlines of the racks, the shelf where the hats were piled up, the bulky hump which was the rail of kaftans. Was it her imagination, or was that some shadowy form which she could see just on the edge of the darkness?

She opened her mouth to call out. Her throat was dry, her breathing harsh. She stopped and closed it again. If there was an intruder there, then the last thing she should do was to let them know where she was. But what could she do? She glanced around desperately, then she spotted the telephone on the desk. Without thinking, Andi reached out instinctively towards the fastest way of getting help. Thank God it's got digital dialling, she thought, as she keyed in the mall security number and put the receiver to her ear. It was several seconds before she realised that the line was completely dead.

Of course! Mr Hamilton had pulled the cord out. The phone was disconnected. She stared at it, stricken, eyes transfixed to the mouthpiece. Her only line of communication, and it was cut off. And with it so was she. She replaced it slowly, and her thoughts came crowding in. Mr Hamilton had quite deliberately wrenched the flex from the wall. Now she was completely isolated, and he knew it. There was no way that she could summon help. And the reason he had done it? Because of the call she had received. Because of the caller whose conversation he had overheard. A woman, an older woman who had tried to warn her.

She could almost hear the voice again in her ear, at this moment. A woman's voice, full of fear. 'Get out. Get out now.' And another voice. That of Mr Hamilton speaking to her this evening echoed in her head. 'I'd be sorry to lose you.' Those words now had a new and sinister meaning. A cold fear clutched at Andi's heart.

There was a faint creak from beyond the open door, as though some person had brushed against a hanger. In a sudden decision Andi reached out and snapped off the office light. Now she felt better. Less exposed. She crept over nearer the door, pressed herself against the wall and waited. Several moments passed.

She tried to think calmly. She must go into the shop. She was trapped if she remained in the office. She had to get past whoever was there and out into the mall. There she could press one of the alarm buttons.

Andi took a deep breath and stepped round the door into the front shop. She took a cautious step forward and immediately a figure came looming at her. Andi gave a small cry and staggered back. It waited, standing directly in front of her, barring her passage to the exit. She raised her hand in defence and the person before her did the same. She dropped her hand in surprise and the hand before her did too. Suddenly Andi's shoulders relaxed and she almost giggled aloud. It was the mirror! She was facing the long cheval-glass with the swivel base which was a feature of the shop. She was staring at her own reflection!

'You idiot!' she said aloud. She made a face at herself. 'Idiot!' she said again and turned to go back to the stockroom.

But . . . she stopped and swung round again. The noise she had heard. The metal grating sound. What had it been? She moved forward a little and looked down towards the shop entrance. The shutter which she had closed and locked earlier was more than halfway up.

Andi's heart began to thud heavily in her chest. Without realising it she took an involuntary step back. Now she was again in front of the mirror. Slowly, slowly, she turned her head. And this time, when she raised her terrified eyes to the glass, she could see not one, but two reflections.

FOURTEEN

Andi's whole body went rigid with fright, and for the briefest second she hesitated. And that was all it took. One second. That was all that was needed. One second later, and she was overpowered from behind.

In that moment, a hooded figure moved at her back and raised its hands. There was a sudden swift rustle and Andi felt something smooth and soft around her neck. She gasped and twisted to the side. But the person behind her was taller and stronger and she was caught fast. Andi struggled desperately, hooking her fingers into the folds of material which was twisted around her neck, trying to pull against the pressure. It was no good. Her delay had lost her the advantage . . . and, she realised . . . her life.

For a single crazy moment her horoscope flashed through her mind. 'Solutions to tricky situations are usually right in front of your eyes.'

In front of her eyes . . . Her own reflection was dissolving in the mirror before her. As she struggled against her attacker she could see this stranger that was herself becoming weaker and weaker . . . The mirror . . . The looking glass . . . in front of her eyes . . .

With a last desperate inspiration Andi fought for her life. In a sudden movement she collapsed completely against her assailant, knocking her head back against their shoulder. They staggered slightly under her weight and leaned forward to tighten their grip. Andi took her chance; she kicked out with her foot as hard as could at the base of the mirror. She heard the crack and a grunt as the mirror pivoted forwards and crashed on her attacker's head. The grip on the scarf loosened as whoever was behind her took the stunning blow.

This time Andi didn't falter. She dug her elbows viciously behind her and ran down the shop, out under the shutter, across the gleaming tiled floor past the sports shop to . . .

Where? Andi shrieked the word aloud. 'Where?'

She slithered to a stop and looked around her in panic. Where should she go? There was no one working on this floor. Probably no one in the whole mall. Except . . . the security guard in the booth on the other side of the door to the underground car park.

Andi raced for the escalator. It was switched off. She stumbled on to the first step. Her shoe caught in the ridged tread and she cried out in pain as her ankle twisted under her. She grasped the guard rail for support and began to descend. It was a long way down. Above her she heard a crash and a thud. The security grid had been pulled up sharply right against the shop roof.

Her attacker had recovered from the blow and was now out of the shop and in the mall. Andi gave a hiccup of fear and limped down a few more steps. She stumbled slightly and recovered her balance.

What were they doing? What was happening? She risked a quick look back. No one followed her. Maybe she was safe. She slowed down a little and walked more carefully. Perhaps whoever had been in the shop was a thief. She had disturbed them and that's why she was attacked. In that case they wouldn't chase her. Surely they would run away?

Was it someone she knew? She hadn't seen their face, only the shadowy outline of their reflection. Someone taller than her, and much stronger. But a thief wouldn't try to kill her, not like that. No, with a sudden shock, Andi realised that whoever had come into the shop earlier had not done so to steal. They had come with the sole intention of doing her harm.

Who was it? She hadn't recognised them, but they didn't know that. They might think that she would be able to identify them. So . . . She glanced back over her shoulder. Why didn't they follow? She halted. Had they somehow got in front of her? Even now, were they waiting in the dark part of the stairwell below her? She moaned a little in fear and indecision. If she shouted now the guard wouldn't hear her. Too far away. Where was the guard anyway? Where was Sedgely? Better to move down, Andi decided, and stepped forward.

She must get to the lower floor. The night security must be somewhere around. Andi limped down a few more steps. Where could Sedgely be? Why did he not come running at the sound of her shriek? And . . . something else struck her. Who had access to the keys of the shop shutters? All the keys and pass cards were kept in the mall office. Andi tried to reason it out. Someone must have been able to get into the office and take the spare key. She glanced around her wildly. Who?

She must keep moving. Not stay still long enough for them to creep up on her. Andi measured the distance she still had to run down to the end of the escalator. If she could get across the lower floor and through the door to the car park, then among the vehicles she would have a better chance. She lifted her foot to step down, when suddenly she was jerked forwards violently. Andi was flung against the side of the barrier and then back again. Someone had started the escalator. It moved, juddered to a halt then slowly it restarted. Only this time it was moving in the opposite directiion. Andi grabbed the edge for support. She was going back up to the top floor!

She braced herself and tried to set her body against the motion of the stairs. She would have to move fast to gain the ground she had lost. Andi twisted round quickly and straightened up, and, as she did so, the trailing ends of the scarf which was still wound round her neck entangled themselves in the sliding stair. She gazed at it for a moment, not understanding completely the situation she was in. Only when the moving stair slid a few further paces did Andi fully appreciate what had happened. Then she started to wrench frantically at the twisted silk around her throat. It was useless. Both ends were now caught in the teeth of the stair mechanism.

Andi cried out in terror. She knew she would never tear herself free. It was part of her own sales pitch, how remarkably strong and hard-wearing these scarves were. She could try as hard as she was able. It didn't matter. She would never get loose. The grey-blue material would not rip or break.

With a small sob of despair Andi fell to her knees. She pushed her hair back from her face and looked upwards to the top floor, to where she was being carried, against her will. She was caught like some animal in a trap, and someone was above, waiting to finish her off.

FIFTEEN

The scarf tightened slowly around Andi's throat as the stair moved up, the hemmed edge cutting cruelly into her skin. She snatched desperately at the flimsy material, trailing it through her fingers, the colour catching the light. It seemed familiar to her. She pulled her head back, trying to gain space. It was no help. She was only making things worse. She grabbed at it again in rage and frustration. Each time she pulled, the knot only became tighter and she was held more closely, just as Leo had been with his bandana earlier when she'd had to help him unfasten it. Andi looked down at the cloth twisted around her neck and tried to see how the knot was tied.

She looked up again hurriedly. The shop signs were coming into view. She only had seconds in which to work. She felt through the scarf with her fingers. There *was* no knot. She almost wept with relief. She had been doing the wrong thing, as usual, rushing in impatiently where careful consideration would have helped her better. If she had taken the time to think it through, she would have realised sooner that the scarf had only been looped around her, so she could have freed herself quite easily. Now she would have to act swiftly. She was almost at the top. She knelt quickly down on the stairs, her face close to their surface. Her eyes were on a level with the treads. She stared at the vicious teeth slotting continuously into the next layer. They moved rhythmically on and on, almost hypnotising her. Working fast she deftly loosened the folds until they draped about her shoulders, then bending her head she twisted under and through and she was free! Free of the throttling influence of the scarf at least . . .

Andi looked up again. The main shopping mall was directly in front of her. She thought quickly. She had wasted enough time. Now she had to get out. She raised herself up unsteadily, turned on the stair and began to make her way downwards, skidding and slithering, back the way she had come. She could not hope to be completely silent, and what's more she no longer cared. Whoever was chasing her must know approximately where she was. They had all the advantages. All she had were the few precious seconds' start which she had gained. They were expecting her to come out at the top floor shortly. Waiting for her, ready to pounce . . .

'Sorry to disappoint you!' she felt like screaming. 'You'll have to wait a little longer. I don't give up so easily.'

She began to feel slightly crazy, as she scrambled desperately one way and the movement of the stairs dragged her in the opposite direction. A mixture of fear and the beginnings of anger.

How could someone play with her like this? Watching her, and stalking her as if she were some hunted animal?

If only she had something to defend herself with. She cast about her. There was nothing within reach. No weapon that she could use. The security guards carried batons at night. The thought repeated in her head. Where was the security guard? Where was Sedgely? Surely it couldn't be him who was chasing her and messing around with the stair mechanism? Yet it had to be someone who knew the mall intimately. And if it wasn't him, then who? And why hadn't he appeared when the stair started up? Hadn't he heard it? She supposed if he was patrolling the furthest side of the mall then he might not.

The next moment a terrific crash resounded through the mall. For a second Andi could hardly imagine what it was. As the echo died away she realised the noise she had heard was the splintering sound of shattering glass. Someone had broken one of the plate-glass windows of the shopfronts. Andi pulled her fringe back from her face and gazed up. Why would anyone break a shop window? It couldn't have been her shop. They had already been inside Moonstone. If they had wanted anything they could have taken it then. So . . . which shop? She tried to think of the shops on either side of her own. On the right hand were two clothes shops and a shoe shop. Then on the left was the sports shop where Tony worked, and next to that a confectioner's. The noise had seemed to come from that direction.

What had they needed so desperately that they had broken the window to get it?

Andi bit her lip as she put more weight on her ankle. It was bruised and swollen, and painful to touch but she had to keep going down the stairs. Still she had no glimpse of anyone. There were dozens of places someone could conceal themselves. The telephone units, the shopping barrows, behind waste bins. She tried not to think. Just keep moving, she told herself. She was more determined than ever now to escape.

Suddenly the escalator slammed to a halt. Andi yelped in fright and stumbled a few more steps. What was going on now?

She looked up and down in panic. Why had they stopped the movement of the stair? Were they watching her from above? Moving closer as she stood there, dithering and shaking? Did they want her at the top or was it a trick to encourage her to move to the lower level where it was dark and someone could easily hide? Conceal themselves quietly and patiently until she started to make her way across the open space. Then . . . they would have her. She would have walked directly into their hands. Which way should she go?

She stayed on the stair, now halfway down, unsure of what to do next. The huge pendulum on the ornate clock swung back and forth. It was the only sound she could hear. That and her own harsh breathing which rasped in her chest. Only minutes had passed since she had fled from the shop. It would be another half an hour before

Mr Hamilton returned. And if the guard was at the far end of the mall, then, she reckoned, it would take him at least fifteen minutes before he was back in this area. There was no one coming to help her. No one at all.

Andi chewed her lip and thought furiously. If she went up, there was more space to run, to run and hide. She could see the fire-alarm button a few short steps away from the other side of the fretwork railing. But . . . the alarm had not gone off when the shop window had been broken, so someone had immobilised it. And whoever had done that could also have immobilised the other alarms.

Her best bet was to go down. It was the quickest way to safety. Down the remaining stairs, across the bottom floor, past the fountain and through the car-park door. She leant on the guard rail to take the weight off her sore ankle and prepared to move again.

At that moment, high above Andi's head, a gloved hand was reaching into the shattered window of the sports shop. From amongst the shards of broken glass it carefully removed the crossbow and arrows.

SIXTEEN

Andi hobbled down another two or three stairs. She could now see over the sides of the escalator. The twelve embroidered Christmas hangings swayed gently around her. The coloured lanterns on the large fir tree had been turned off. The tinsel and foil decorations gleamed dully, their gaiety mocking her. At the very top was the fairy with her raised wand and permanent smile. She'll smile like that tomorrow, Andi thought, in exactly the same way, whether I live or die.

She brushed her hair back with her hands and tucked it behind her ears. 'I must stay calm,' she whispered to herself. 'I must stay calm.'

There had been no further noise or movement since the breaking of the window and the escalator stopping a few moments ago. She hoped they had given up and gone away. Being unable to prevent her from reaching the bottom floor they might know that she would soon be beyond their grasp. Better that they should leave too, and as quickly as possible. Then she would never know who her attacker was. And they must want it to stay that way. A shiver passed over her, and a sudden lurch of nausea, as she realised that she must know whoever it was that was out to do her harm. It had to be a person she would recognise. That's why they were taking care to stay out of sight, hoping that she hadn't known who they were when they had attacked her in the shop earlier.

There was an orange light shining above the door to the car park. The rest of the ground floor was in shadow. The café chairs stacked on the table made strange shapes and patterns in the half-dark. Was there someone there, lurking among the furniture or behind the counter? Keeping her in view until she made her next move? Andi bent her head low and listened for a long moment. She could hear the murmuring sound of the water in the ornamental fountain, the bubbling of the tiny whirlpools and the hiss of the waterjets.

If only she could see her attacker. It was the fear of the unknown which was turning her muscles to liquid, causing her arms and legs to tremble and shake. She breathed in and out slowly a couple of times to steady herself, ever-conscious that the seconds were ticking away. She was losing time, and her enemy was gaining with every moment that passed. Gathering their strength, using the delay to think and plan . . . what?

Andi heard a faint creak and then a soft swishing noise. She raised her head and concentrated. Was it the door to the service stairs opening and closing? She couldn't tell exactly what she had heard. Did the falling water in the fountain make that noise? She could see it now quite clearly from her position on the stair. The coins which had been tossed in for luck glinted from the depths of the pool. She needed luck now.

But, she inclined her head slightly, there *was* another noise. She could just hear it, a faint echo on the rim of her hearing, the barest whisper of a sound. Andi couldn't make up her mind what it was. It was so frustrating to be isolated like this with no cover, she thought. Stuck out in the open in such a way, she presented a prime target to whoever was stalking her. She gasped as a sudden picture of herself in the light, and her pursuer watching her from the darkness, came into her mind. At once and instinctively she crouched down quickly on the stairs.

Just as she did so, a hard sharp clack sounded in the mall. It was like no sound she had ever heard before. There was a whizzing rasp, and an arrow sliced the air centimetres from her shoulder. It thudded hard into one of the ornamental pillars which rose between the floors and buried itself deep in the wood.

Andi screamed in terror and, lurching forwards, she tripped over the hem of her skirt and fell. She tumbled down a few stairs flinging her hands out to stop herself. She lay sprawled and winded for several seconds, then grabbed the guard rail and hauled herself partly upright. She couldn't believe it. She stared at the arrow still quivering just centimetres away from her head. The wood surrounding it was splintered and broken where the point lay firmly embedded. It could easily have been her.

Suddenly her calm broke. 'Who are you?' she shrieked. 'Who are you? Why are you doing this?' Her voice bounced against the empty shops, echoed round the frescoed walls, and was lost in the glass roof . . . 'are you, are you, are you . . .' The hysterical refrain faded to nothing. Silence.

Andi looked up. The arrow had come from above, and, she shuddered, whoever had done it was probably preparing to fire a second. Now she knew what the noise was that she had heard earlier. It was explained, the unrecognisable sounds had followed a pattern. The click of the arrow being slid into place, the teasing back of the bolt of the crossbow. And even as the thought took shape in her mind she heard it again. Her eyes widened as there came a neat click from behind and above her. Then the sound of the bolt being drawn back. She would have to make a run for it. Now.

Andi gathered the folds of her long print skirt in her hand, straightened up a little and set herself for a final desperate sprint to the exit door. She gave one last glance about, then tensing herself to bear the pain in her ankle, she took off down the last few stairs and across the mall.

There came another sharp snap of sound, and she veered to one side and ran on. An arrow zinged past her and clattered to the floor ahead of her. A sob broke in her throat. Whoever was aiming at her was a good shot.

Andi reached the door, and moaning with relief she clutched at the handle. Her fingers were wet with perspiration and the metal bar slipped from her grasp. She could almost see the crossbow being reloaded, the wire stretched across ready for release. She wiped her hands hurriedly on her skirt and grabbed again. It remained stuck. She twisted the handle the other way. It didn't move. The door held fast. She flung herself against it. It was no use. The door had been locked securely.

Andi was trapped inside the mall.

SEVENTEEN

With a small whimper of fear Andi slumped down against the steel door. Her gaze darted frantically here and there. There was nowhere for her to go, nowhere to run.

Time. She needed time. If only she could avoid getting caught for a bit longer. Each moment that she was free increased her chances of staying alive. Her dad would call for her eventually. If she could keep running until then, she would be safe. She usually met him at the main exit door. He would come looking for her if she didn't show up on time. She had to keep one step ahead until he arrived.

Her eyes searched desperately around her. She caught sight of the arrow lying on the floor of the mall and she realised again the danger she was in by staying still. She pushed herself away from the door and, bending almost double, she scurried over to the café. She crouched down amongst the furniture in her temporary shelter. It was a false security, she knew. Where the café was situated on the lower level it could be seen from almost any point on the upper floor. The tables and chairs were bamboo and her bright red top would show clearly through them. But at least it gave some protection from a crazy person with a crossbow.

And this person *must* be crazy, she reckoned. What possible reason could anyone have for wishing to harm her? This wasn't a spur of the moment attack. She was being chased, hunted down like a wild animal.

As if on cue another arrow zinged through the air and rebounded off a table a little to her left. Andi ducked. Well, she thought grimly, at least on this occasion she had seen where it had come from. From the top floor. If only she could see who it was. She changed her position quickly, scuttling between the chairs, but her pursuer moved too. She saw the brief outline of a shadow above her. And then she saw something else. The entrance to the loading bay.

Andi's heart started to thud. Had she enough time to reach it before the person above her came down either the escalator or the stairs? She had only been in there once before to check for missing goods, but she knew it was also used as a storeroom. If she could get herself through that door then she might find something to barricade it with. She pushed her fringe out of her eyes and sized up the distance she would have to run. The sides of her face and her back were wet with perspiration and she could hardly keep her chin still. She placed her hands on the floor to steady herself. Then she squatted on her heels and waited for her opportunity. And waited.

It was stalemate, Andi thought. She couldn't

move for fear of being picked off in the open, but whoever it was didn't want their identity revealed so they had to stay out of sight. What was the next step and who would be the first to move?

Directly above Andi's head someone was opening the main electricity control panel. Strong fingers grasped the fuse switch for the lights and pulled it down. Every light on both floors went out at once. Andi raised her head in bewilderment. What had happened? Every single light couldn't have fused simultaneously. It was another trick to demoralise her, another way to catch her out. The emergency lamps burned dully on the walls and some illumination came through the glass dome from outside, enough for the archer to pick out her brightly coloured top as a target.

And now the landscape around her had changed. The furniture among which she hid, instead of offering protection, became hulking monster outlines crowding in on her.

Suddenly, from above, came the sound of running feet. Someone was racing on the stairs, boots thudding, taking the steps two at a time, trying to get to her before she could move.

Andi got up and flung herself forwards. Her sight was badly affected by the sudden darkness. She could see rainbow spots dancing across her vision but she ran on, her hands held out in front of her. She reached the door. Hair swinging wildly behind her she hauled it open. It slipped from her hand and banged against the wall.

Behind her she heard a heart-chilling yell of rage and frustration. She crashed the door shut behind her.

Andi grabbed the first thing to hand and dragged it towards her. Her breath was coming in great ragged sobs as she pushed it firmly against her side of the door. She turned round . . . anything else? She stopped in mid-action, arm stretched out. There was a figure in the storeroom. Taller than her, stronger, standing just behind her.

'NO!' Andi yelled and threw herself down.

It didn't change position. She blinked in the gloomy half-darkness and saw several more similar figures. She sat up at once, almost crying with relief.

'Dummies!' she shrieked and started to laugh hysterically. She collapsed on to the box beside her. There was a group of shop-window mannequins lined up in the corner. She wiped her face with her sleeve and stood up. She hurried over and grabbed the first one.

'Might as well be useful,' she told it, and stuck it on top of her box. She searched around for a few more items and piled them up too, then she stood back and looked at her fortifications. Now she felt a lot better. She peered at her watch. What time was it? The emergency lights glowed softly and she could barely see the hands. She groaned. Unbelievably, only ten minutes had passed.

She could look for a weapon while she waited. She started to rummage around. Anything would do. A piece of wood, a pole or stick of any sort. She bent down to search under a low shelf, and as she did so a voice whispered right in her ear.

'Andi,' it said softly. 'I'm coming to get you.'

EIGHTEEN

Andi screamed. A piercing wail that climbed higher and higher. Her whole body started to shake and the piece of wood which she had taken hold of slipped out of her grasp. She tried to get control of herself. There's no one here, she said to herself. No one. I checked. There's no one in this room. She pressed her knuckles hard against her mouth.

'I'm coming for you, Andi. You can't escape.' The low voice rolled around the room like a giant's whisper.

Andi screwed up her eyes and looked back at the door. It was shut tight. Nothing had been moved. Where then was the source of the noise? Suddenly she noticed two speakers fixed on the far wall. It was coming through the PA system. Turned up to a deafening pitch, the sound, hugely distorted, reached into every corner of the room.

'Not long to wait, Andi. I'll be with you soon.'

Andi covered her ears with her hands but still it came through. The words crawling spider-like all over her skin, brushing her face like cobwebs, coming closer, sounding all around her.

'Andi. There is no way out. No way out at all.'

Another great shudder of fear set Andi's body trembling again. She had to stop this, she told herself. It was what they wanted. They were trying to frighten her into a state of absolute collapse. Well, she wouldn't give them the satisfaction. She clenched her fists, nails digging deep into her palms.

'No escape from me.' The words vibrated through the room. 'No way out. No way out.'

But there is, Andi thought determinedly. Yes, there is. She remembered the initial reason she had run this way. The loading bay. It was situated at the furthest end of this area. There must be some mechanism, she reasoned, for raising and lowering the hoist. So she should be able to gain access to the section of the underground car park where the delivery vans came and went.

'Andi.'

She raised her head and listened carefully. She had heard that voice before.

'You're caught, Andi. There's nowhere to go.'

The voice was familiar. It was someone she had spoken to, had a conversation with, and recently. But the volume control was so high that it transformed it completely. She could not recognise it.

'Andi . . . I'm coming for you.'

Something else . . . Andi thought, as her name was spoken again. Something not quite right about the tone as it vibrated through the air, unnaturally hoarse and sibilant.

'Andi . . .'

It was playing with her, teasing her. Trying to break her down, to force her into such an hysterical state that she couldn't cope, wouldn't be able to function.

She hurried between the stacks. The transit area . . . there it was ahead of her. The terrible voice had stopped. Just as well, it was almost more than she could bear. Now the silence was closing in on her, menacing in a more subtle way. What were they doing? What was being planned for her now? It doesn't matter, she told herself. They're too late. Nothing can stop me now. A few short steps to freedom. Within minutes I will be on the main street. They can't follow me there.

Still . . . There was a nagging feeling at the back of her mind. Whoever her enemy was had a complete knowledge of the mall and its workings. Therefore they would know about the loading bay. Know where it was located and have already worked out where she was going. And might be . . . Andi slowed her steps . . . might even now be moving to head her off.

It was directly in front of her. The shop staff rarely came here. It was one of the security guards' jobs to oversee the deliveries. Andi could see it now, the gridded hatch with the control panel to one side. The hoist lay empty.

A knowledge of the mall. The thought was in her head again. Mr Sedgely, the security guard. He would know where the light switches were and how to work the PA system. Creepy Sedgely, who watched people. But that wasn't so strange.

It was what security people were supposed to do. Yet . . . he should be on duty, so where was he at this moment?

Andi made the last few paces to the loading bay, and the answer to her question lay sprawled at her feet. His hands were flung out above his head as though he had fallen while trying to protect himself. His eyes were closed and the skin beneath them was of a grey chalky pallor.

'Mr Sedgely!' Andi gasped.

She knelt down beside him and felt for a pulse. Nothing. She put her hand on the side of his neck. His body felt cold to touch. They had practised first aid and accident-recovery techniques often enough in school for Andi to appreciate that he needed more than basic attention. She took her hand away from behind his head. Her fingers had blood on them. Whoever had struck him down had done it viciously and from behind.

She felt tears come into her eyes. He hadn't deserved this. To be left like a discarded package, dumped in a corner. The packages. She recalled Pam had come down here with him to check on her parcel. The one she had been expecting that hadn't arrived. The one she had been so anxious and annoyed about. Where was she now? Was she implicated in this in some way? Or was she lying like some broken doll in another corner? And if she was, then who was the person in the mall? Who had been following her around, intent on murder?

'I'm getting out of here before it's too late.'

She spoke aloud. She raised her eyes to her one means of escape from the mall and, as she did, suddenly there was a slow grinding noise. To begin with she didn't understand. Then as it came to her, as the first glimmer of comprehension dawned as to what the noise might be, some part of her refused to accept it. To have got so close, to be almost there, on the threshold of freedom, it was as if her brain wouldn't allow herself to think that she could be thwarted. But she knew. She had left it too late. Had delayed too long. The noise she now heard was the sound of the hoist being raised.

Someone was coming up. From below ground level. In seconds they would arrive right in the storeroom beside her. And where could she go? Behind her was a blocked exit, the one that she herself had barricaded. This time she couldn't move. She had no strength left to run.

Andi stared straight ahead in fascinated terror. The voice had been right. She was caught fast. There was no way out for her now. No way at all.

NINETEEN

Andi slowly backed away from the body of Mr Sedgely as she heard the hoist rising. It slid into position on a level with the loading bay and came to a halt. The figure crouching down inside stepped from the ledge into the room.

Andi moved carefully, quietly retracing her steps to the end of the shelf units and watched. A cold chill had settled on her heart. Despite the gloom, and the fact that the person's back was to her, she knew. Knew before he straightened up so that the small amount of light that there was fell on his face showing his features clearly to her. Before he even spoke her name . . .

'Andi?'

It was a whisper. But . . . not the nasty taunting voice of earlier. This time low and urgent.

'Andi?'

She crept softly along the stacks to the entrance door. She gripped the box and tried to move it gently to one side. If she could just make enough room to get the door open a fraction . . . only a tiny space would be needed for her to edge through. She could hear his footsteps padding behind her. She lifted the dummy down carefully to set it to one side . . . and it slipped from her trembling fingers.

'Who's there?' His voice was sharper now. 'Come out, whoever you are!'

Andi didn't care now about the noise she made. She thrust the rest of the boxes to one side and reached for the door handle. To her surprise it moved as she touched it, and the door was pushed in against her. She jumped back in alarm. There was someone on the other side. She hesitated, unsure of what to do.

'Andi,' came a cry at her back.

Andi turned to face Leo.

'You're all right,' he said.

There was relief in his voice. How could he be so deceitful? Pretending to be concerned. Andi saw the wooden stave which she had dropped earlier. She picked it up from the low shelf beside her.

'Stay back,' she commanded him. Her voice came out as a croak. 'Stay back.' She held it up in front of her.

'What's the matter?' He stopped at once. 'What's going on?'

'Yes,' echoed a voice from the door. 'What is going on?'

Andi whirled round. 'Pam!' she said. She had never been so relieved to see anyone in her life.

'Pam. I'm so glad to see you!'

Pam pushed the door wide and came into the storeroom. 'All the lights are out in the mall,' she said. 'I can't get them on. Where is Sedgely?'

'Lying over there.' Andi nodded in the direction of the corner where she had found the guard's body. 'I think someone has killed him.'

'Killed him!' said Pam.

'Are you sure?' asked Leo. 'Why would anyone want to kill Sedgely?'

'I don't know why.' Andi could hear her own voice becoming higher and higher. 'Someone has been trying to kill me too.'

She was aware that both Pam and Leo were looking at her strangely. They exchanged puzzled glances.

'It's true,' said Andi. 'Why do you think I barricaded myself in here?' She turned to Pam. 'Didn't you notice anyone outside in the mall?'

Pam shook her head. 'No, but I've only just returned. I had driven halfway home before I realised I'd forgotten something.'

'There was someone out there earlier,' said Andi desperately. 'They attacked me in the shop, tried to strangle me.' She touched her neck as she remembered. 'With one of the long silk scarves.'

'I wouldn't try to hurt you,' said Leo quietly. 'I would never harm you, Andi.'

'Then what are you doing here?' demanded Pam. She moved closer to Andi.

'I came back . . .' Leo hesitated. 'I wanted to see Andi, to talk to her.'

'You could have done that earlier,' said Pam. She turned to Andi. 'I told you there was something odd about him.'

'Why did you come up in the hoist?' said Andi. Her voice shook. Any second now and she would be in tears.

103

'Because the door from the car park had been locked,' said Leo. 'I went back outside to try the service entrance, and then I saw all the lights go out. I thought something was wrong. This was the only way I could think of to get in.'

'I've just come through that door,' Pam said quietly. 'It was open a moment ago.'

Andi looked at Leo. He *must* have been the person who was chasing her. When she had shut herself in the storeroom he had unlocked the car-park door and run round to the hoist to cut her off. A curtain of despair descended on her. She dropped the wooden stick she had been holding and put her hands over face.

'Why?' said Leo suddenly.

Andi lifted her head and stared at him.

'Why?' he repeated. 'Why would I attack you? What reason would I have to do such a thing?'

'I don't know,' said Andi. She was sobbing now. 'I don't know. There are already two, maybe three, missing teenagers. Who knows why somebody does something like that?'

Leo's face went white. 'Andi,' he said. 'That's got nothing to do with me. You don't really think that I would do something like that?' He stretched out his hand to her. 'Do you?'

Trust your instinct.

Andi looked again at Leo.

Trust your instinct.

Firm fingers dug into her arm. It was Pam. She bent swiftly and picked up the stick which Andi had let fall.

'Let's get out of here!' she said. 'He tried to

strangle you with his own scarf. He's crazy.' She grabbed Andi's wrist and dragged her through the door into the mall. Andi turned to look back over her shoulder. She could no longer see Leo in the dim light behind her.

'Come on,' said Pam urgently, and pulled Andi towards the stairs. 'We've got to get away from him while we can.'

Andi stumbled along beside Pam to the foot of the escalator. 'Where are we going?' she asked, looking at the shadows around them.

'Up,' said Pam firmly. 'He'll be waiting for us in the car-park if we go that way. We'll use one of the emergency exits upstairs.'

They were now on the stair that Andi had come down to the lower level on. It seemed an impossible struggle for her. The slightest pressure on her ankle was unbearably painful, and she was exhausted and drained by fear. She was never going to make it.

'Stop!' yelled a voice behind them.

They both turned. There was a figure below them on the stairs. It was Leo. He had started to climb up after them. He was stronger and fitter and he was gaining rapidly.

TWENTY

'Keep going.' Pam pushed Andi in front of her.

'I can't,' said Andi. She fell on to her knees on the stairs. 'I can't,' she whispered again.

They were almost at the place on the stairs where the scarf had caught in the treads. Andi stared at it, just above her head, the trails of blue and grey still bunched together. Something stirred in her memory. She had sold that scarf only an hour ago. The last one in that particular pattern.

'Leo's scarf,' she said aloud.

'Exactly,' said Pam grimly. 'Now get up. We have to move.'

Andi dragged herself to her feet. 'No,' she said. She moved up a few steps so that she was above Pam. 'No,' she shouted out loudly. 'Both of you stand still. I have to work something out.'

Leo stopped a few stairs below. Andi saw his eyes, clear blue, holding hers.

Trust your instinct.

'What is it, Andi?' he asked. 'What do you need to know?'

'Nothing,' said Pam. She leant forwards, her eyes glittering. 'It's his scarf. You recognised it. You don't need any more proof.'

'Leo, where is your scarf?' Andi called out. 'The one I sold you earlier?'

Leo felt in his jacket pocket. 'It's not there,' he said. 'I must have left it somewhere . . . I stopped to speak to Pam. Don't you remember?' he asked Pam. 'I told you I'd just bought it. I must have dropped it, or left it down – '

'He's lying,' Pam interrupted. 'He's trying to cover up his guilt. You know it's his scarf. You said so yourself.'

'Yes I did, didn't I,' said Andi. 'But . . . then . . . so did you.'

Pam's eyes narrowed. She watched Andi carefully.

'In the storeroom,' Andi went on, 'a few moments ago. You said that Leo tried to strangle me with his own scarf. That's the phrase you used: "his own scarf".' Andi took a step down towards Pam and looked her full in the face. 'How did you know, Pam? How did you know that the scarf that had been pulled round my neck, the one that's here on the stairs, was Leo's?'

'I . . .' Pam hesitated.

'There's only one way that you could possibly have known,' said Andi, 'isn't there? And . . . another thing, you said you left the mall and came back for something. What was it?'

'Look,' said Leo. He pulled a voucher from his top pocket. 'This is my park-and-pay ticket. It proves I left and came back. Where's *your* ticket, Pam?'

The speed at which Pam moved surprised Leo and Andi. She lifted the wooden stave which she still held, and struck Leo hard across the face. He cried out and his legs crumpled beneath him. Then she turned like a cornered animal on Andi.

'You've ruined everything,' she spat at her. 'This whole thing took me months to set up. Everything was perfect. The delivery, the distribution. No one suspected anything. I'd found the perfect place to get the stuff out. In among crowds of people, where nobody notices another stranger. Except you. You, with your spying snooping eyes. And him, hanging about all the time.' She kicked Leo with her foot. 'And you encouraging him. Otherwise he would never have come back for you. You would have disappeared. Another missing teenager. Who cares? Now I'm going to have to move on. And it's all your fault.'

'I don't even know what you're talking about,' said Andi. 'You're the one that's crazy.' And she was, Andi suddenly realised. The girl before her was shaking uncontrollably. Her eyes were staring in her head, her skin had a waxy sweat on it.

'Only because you held up my stuff, you stupid fool! You took the wrong parcel. The one you opened and left on the shop counter was meant for me.'

'The bath salts?' said Andi. She remembered now, rummaging for the invoice. The powder spilling from the little packets. All the little packets . . . 'Drugs,' said Andi. 'You're a dealer. And,' she looked at Pam in horror, at the nervous tremors running through her body, the desperate wild look on her face, 'you're an addict too.'

'When Sedgely told me that you must have my parcel I realised I had to deal with both of you,' Pam said. 'I knew it would be opened, and as soon as Jack Hamilton returned I was finished. I pretended to leave and then came back and crept up on Sedgely.' She laughed. 'He had no idea at all, he was actually singing as he swept up the storeroom. One good hard blow and he fell. And that . . .' Pam advanced towards Andi on the stairs, 'that only left you. I got the shutter keys from the office, and as soon as I saw my packets strewn all over your shop counter I decided I must silence you. If I could get rid of you quickly then I had a chance at least.' She gripped the wooden stick in both hands. 'It's still not too late for me,' she said. Pam drew the stick back to strike again.

'Don't,' said Andi.

She should have felt fear or hatred. This person had tried to kill her. But she didn't, she couldn't. She felt half sorry for this pathetic trembling human being in front of her. Andi sidestepped Pam and grabbed the stick. With a swift confident movement she wrenched it out of her grip. Pam reached for her, nails clawing at Andi's face. Andi pushed her away. She had to reach Leo. See if he was all right.

Pam ran further up the stairs. She turned at the top. 'You think you've won,' she said. 'Well, you haven't. I gave you one prediction before. Well, here's another one.' She pointed her finger at Andi. 'I predict,' she hissed, 'that you are going to die.'

TWENTY-ONE

Andi scarcely heard Pam's vindictive screech. She was bent over Leo who lay still and pale on the stairs. She brushed his hair back from his face. The blow had caught him across the forehead and the skin was broken and weeping blood.

'Leo,' Andi whispered. 'Leo.'

She laid her hand on his cheek. It was quite cold. As cold as Sedgely had been in the storeroom. Andi shivered as she remembered him lying there, and the terrible voice crowding all around them both. Now she knew why it had sounded so strange and unnatural. It was Pam disguising the sound, pitching it lower to sound more like a man's.

Andi looked up above her head. Where was Pam now? She must have gone to take her parcel from the shop . . . and then what? Surely she would leave by another exit. But she couldn't, Andi realised, she wouldn't be able to. The emergency exits were secured at night. And Pam would know that, Andi thought. She had obviously taken great care to find out all about the workings of the mall. She had been in the best position to do that, sitting at the stairs watching everybody, talking to the shopkeepers, the cleaners, the security. She would know everything she needed to know to get out, or . . . to plan her revenge.

'Leo.' Andi spoke his name again, this time more firmly. 'Come on,' she said to him. 'We have got to move. We can't stay here. It's too dangerous.'

Leo moaned and moved his head. Andi put one hand behind his neck and one under his shoulder.

'You'll have to help me,' she told him. 'I can't possibly lift you by myself.'

His eyelids opened and he moaned again. He looked at Andi and smiled. She felt her eyes fill with tears.

'You're alive,' she said.

'I think so,' said Leo. He grinned at her. 'I've been trying for weeks to get your arms around my neck. I didn't know I'd have to go as far as this to do it.'

Tears were running down Andi's cheeks. She didn't bother wiping them away. She didn't care.

'Why didn't you say something?' she asked him. 'I mean, most guys just leave their telephone number,' she joked. 'They don't climb up through hoists.'

Leo got slowly to his feet. 'I did try,' he said. 'Despite what my horoscope may say, I am quite shy. There were always tons of people around you. And then, I tried to make conversation with you to find out your star sign and ended up buying every soap and scented oil that you stocked.'

'Was that what that was all about!' exclaimed Andi as she helped him to his feet. 'I thought you had a dozen girlfriends!'

Leo leaned on her shoulder and rubbed his head. 'Why did Pam hit me?' he said. 'Why did she attack you and Sedgely?'

'She's a drug dealer,' said Andi, 'and we were just about to find out. Her sketching was a front. People could come and go at her table quite naturally all the time. I did wonder why she was never much interested in custom for her portraits.'

Leo looked around him. 'Where is she anyway?' he asked.

'Right above your head,' came a hard brittle voice.

Andi and Leo looked up. Pam stood at the edge of the upper guard rail. She had something in her hand. It was the blowtorch from the glass-ornament booth.

'I told you that you weren't going to get off so easily,' she shouted.

'What's she up to?' whispered Andi.

'I don't know,' said Leo. 'Pam,' he called out, 'there's nothing more you can do. It would be best if you just left.'

'I am leaving,' Pam replied. 'But you're not!' She turned up the burner of the blowlamp and leant out over the decorated barrier railing.

'Pam! Don't!' yelled Andi.

It was too late. The flame from the torch caught the edge of the hanging picture. In seconds it had ignited, the fire spreading up and across its length. Pam gave a wild yell, ran a few metres further on and set fire to the next one.

Leo and Andi held on to each other. They couldn't move, paralysed with fright. The cords securing the first hanging burnt through and it fell, slowly twisting as it went, down into the lower level. A shower of sparks flared out and settled on the Christmas tree. Andi's eyes were wide with shock, the bright light of the burning decorations reflected in them. Leo turned his head, watching Pam as she circled above them on her path of destruction. All the hangings were now alight, flames rapidly scorching through them, licking hungrily at the wooden beams and stair supports.

It was the smoke, starting to billow up from the ground floor, catching in Andi's throat and making her cough, that brought her suddenly to her senses. 'Leo!' she cried. 'We'll be burnt alive if we stay here!'

As she spoke a large molten piece of Christmas decoration shrivelled and fell on her, brushing past her hair and settling on her skirt. It stuck on the printed cotton and a black hole appeared, spreading, widening, as Andi gazed at it, stupified. She could feel the heat on her skin, blistering, intense.

Suddenly Leo was slapping at it with his hands, smothering the red angry glow. The two of them stared at each other, then without speaking they grabbed each other's hands and started down the escalator.

The fire was all around them. A roaring, raging

monster that would not let them pass. The bamboo tables and chairs were alight. The Christmas tree and the lanterns. Andi saw the tinsel blacken on the green branches, and the face of the fairy at the very top of the tree crumple and melt in the heat. They weren't going to make it. The smoke was in their lungs, thick and dense. There was no clear air to breathe.

Andi pushed her hair back. It was singeing on her head, frazzled in the intense heat. She could hardly see now. Only the firm grip of Leo's hand in hers gave her strength.

Was this how it was meant to be? To end up like this, the victim of a frenzied attack? It couldn't be. The picture pinned on her bedroom wall flashed into her mind. The arrow. Her prediction, Sagittarius, the fire sign. The luminous glow of the flames encircling her face in the portrait.

Was this how she was meant to die? Had it been foretold? A deadly horoscope turned horrorscope?

TWENTY-TWO

All Andi's thoughts and fears were a frantic jumble inside her mind. And Leo's must be the same, she thought. Unable to see or think. They were on the ground floor, and some way from the stairs. But going where? In which direction lay the storeroom and safety? Too far, Andi decided. They wouldn't have enough time to reach it before they would be engulfed. She could feel her strength draining away. She couldn't cope with this situation.

And above the crackling of the ever-devouring flames Andi could hear another noise. Echoing round the walls, a horrible, and totally terrifying sound. It was Pam laughing. She really is out of her mind, Andi thought. Pam's addiction explained a lot. Her mood swings. The constant irritation and anxiety. The high-pitched shriek which now sounded through the mall came from the throat of a crazed person.

Then Andi was aware of another sound. Directly beside her. Not loud, but persistent, a hissing and bubbling near her feet. She grabbed Leo's arm. 'The fountain!' she cried. 'Leo, we're right beside the waterfall!'

It hardly took a second before he understood. He bent quickly and scooped her up in his arms. Then he clambered over the miniature wall and dropped down into the water. They crouched down as low as they could in the ornamental pool. Leo took Andi's face in both of his hands.

'Listen,' he told her. 'We can't stay here. We would choke to death. We have to make a run for it. Agreed?'

Andi put her hands over his and laced her fingers through his own. 'Agreed,' she whispered in reply.

She was terrified. She looked up at the mall arching over her. The huge clock which seemed to be ticking her life away, and higher still to the glass dome, above which were the sky and the stars. All she could see was acrid swirling smoke.

Leo pulled off his jacket and soaked it thoroughly in the water. 'Wet your hair,' he told her, 'as much as you can.' He draped the jacket around both their heads and shoulders. They clambered back over the wall. Leo put one arm firmly around Andi's waist, and with the other he held his jacket across their faces. Then together they ran desperately in the direction of the storeroom.

It seemed a longer distance than before to Andi as they stumbled forwards in the dark. Despite the wetness of the cloth, she could feel heat on her face and neck. Scorching and suffocating. She was sure her skirt was on fire. The floor tiles were searing hot through the soles of her shoes.

At one point she slipped and almost fell. Leo grabbed her and hauled cruelly on her arm. He grunted something, but she didn't hear. She knew she must not stop, could not stop. If she did, it wasn't her life alone that was at risk. Some small part of her understood that Leo wouldn't leave her. If she faltered, then he would also perish. And finally, when she thought about it later, she was sure that was what kept her going, made her keep walking, half-running, when she wanted to give up, when she thought she couldn't take one other step. Lungs bursting, she suddenly felt in front of her the handle of the door leading to the loading bay.

And then they were through it to the other side, smoke curling after them, seeking out the gaps and following. But they could see the hoist and their exit to freedom. Then they heard above everything the scream of a fire siren and the sound of a tender drawing up outside.

Leo insisted she went down first, bundling her quickly into the hoist despite her protests. And then he followed. The car park was filled almost at once with firemen, putting on their masks and running out their hoses. She was separated from Leo in the confusion. He had taken the firemen back inside to locate Sedgely. And then her dad was there, pushing through the crowds, his face grey with fear. Andi flung her arms around his neck and burst into tears.

At the hospital later she saw Sedgely being brought in. The paramedics had been working on him. To Andi's relief she saw that his eyes were open and he gave her a weak smile as he was carried from an ambulance.

Jack Hamilton was waiting for her when eventually the doctors had finished and she was allowed to go. He took Andi's hands and then pulled her close and hugged her tightly.

'There's someone I want you to meet,' he said. He took her to where a woman sat waiting. 'This is my wife,' he said. 'I've brought her here to apologise to you.'

Much later that night when Andi was tucked up in bed after being discharged from casualty and interviewed by the police, she explained to Liz.

'It was his wife who made the phone call. To try to scare me away from the shop. She was jealous of any young girl working for Jack, and she used to do that all the time. That was why he didn't want me to answer the telephone, and why he never kept any staff. The last girl was so frightened that she didn't go home. When she was reported missing in the newspaper Jack went to the police himself and reported his wife. The girl turned up at a friend's house. Then he made his wife come and speak to me.'

'What about the girl found in the wood?' asked Liz.

'They think she OD'd on some drugs. Probably the same source as Pam's. That was some strange stuff she had.'

'And Pam . . .?' Liz asked.

Andi shuddered. The last thing she remembered before her dad had arrived at the mall and taken her to hospital was the paramedics going past her with a covered body on a stretcher.

There was a knock on Andi's bedroom door. Andi's father came in.

'I'm going,' said Liz, getting up.

'Actually I've brought another visitor,' said Andi's dad.

Leo stepped into the room behind him.

'I'm definitely going,' said Liz.

'Ten minutes, young man,' said Andi's dad. 'No more.'

Liz gave Andi a quick hug. 'Catch you later,' she winked at her, 'and hear the gossip.'

'Bye,' said Andi.

Leo sat carefully on the edge of the bed.

'Are you OK?' asked Andi.

'A bit bruised and some minor burns.' He waved a bandaged hand under Andi's nose. 'How about you?'

'I'm fine.' Andi smiled happily at him. 'A bit shaky, but I think I'll get over it.'

'Will you go back?' he asked her.

'To Moonstone?' asked Andi. Jack Hamilton had asked her that same question. 'Yes,' she said firmly. 'It hasn't put me off. I've still got the window to sort out.'

She caught sight of her portrait prediction still pinned to her wall. She reached up and took it down. It had certainly spooked her. Perhaps there was some truth in premonitions. She had been disturbed by it from the very beginning. There was no real explanation for the way she had felt in the mall, the restlessness and unease that came over her when she had been near Pam. Or perhaps there was. Maybe an extra power existed that just couldn't be rationalised.

'I'm not going to pay any attention to predictions ever again,' she told Leo.

'Absolutely not?' asked Leo. He looked into her eyes.

'Definitely not,' said Andi.

'That's a pity,' said Leo. Using his uninjured hand he took a few wisps of Andi's hair and stroked it back from her face. 'I was going to make a prediction, and I hoped it would come true.'

'What is it?' asked Andi.

'I predict that I'm going to kiss you,' said Leo.

William Bedford

THE JOY-RIDERS

The thing with danger is, you've got to keep going on . . . you have to keep pushing at the limits.

The brothers Grim Jo called them. It seemed a suitable enough name for Rainbow and Ash, teenage brothers who had been bred on a life of crime, rebels who knew all the limits but just ignored them. After all, isn't that what joyriding is all about, twocking or 'taking without owner's consent'? Jo, like every other kid, never meant to get involved but when they threaten her with blackmail, she has no choice – the forfeit is to become one of them.

Yet she never thought she would enjoy it, or begin to need the exhilaration that fear provides – like Rainbow and Ash, the danger of living on the edge becomes the only thing worth living for.

Then the final dare comes and what do you do when you're racing along a promenade, hurtling towards a ten foot drop, with only a railing between you and the sea, when the speed is 80 mph but every second seems a century long, when escape isn't an option . . .

Maeve Henry

A GIFT FOR A GIFT

Since her father left, things at home are impossible for
Fran. Her mother has given up trying to keep the
family together and Fran is left to look after the house
and her two younger brothers.

One night, in despair and anger, Fran storms out of
the house and seeks refuge in what seems to be an
empty house. But there she meets the strange and elu-
sive Michael, who has the power to grant her any
wish but who, in return, insists on a gift of his own
choosing – that Fran will stay with him in this life and
beyond.

A strong and beautifully written story of despair,
hope and self-realisation.

Frances Usher

FACE TO FACE

'It was as if I had an enemy somewhere who had picked me out – just me –'

Nick's dreams are driving him mad – running down endless corridors where he is haunted by the laughter of a girl with dark hair. Are the dreams a warning that destiny will bring him together with the unknown girl in a terrible way? And then Nick sees the girl on a school bus . . .

Obsessed with her image, Nick is determined to contact her, but his journey leads him to a discovery he could never have imagined . . .

"a compelling psychological thriller."

The Guardian